"Do I Know You?"

Cassie had recognized him right away. That smile, that handsome face.

Cassie stood frozen for a moment, taking note of the man Jake Griffin had become. From the look of him, he'd done a great job of keeping his body intact. Yards of hard muscle and his sure-enough attitude probably kept the ladies lining up.

Jake Griffin had been the first boy to disappoint her…leading to a world-class string of bad choices when it came to the opposite sex. Cassie had a penchant for attracting troubled men.

"I'd better get going," she said. The fact that he didn't recognize her did nothing for her ego.

"Hate to let you go before I've figured out how I know you," Jake said.

But Cassie was praying that he wouldn't remember her. If she hadn't known him, she might have stayed to chat with the handsome calf roper. But she did know him, and alarm bells were ringing loud and clear in her head.

Dear Reader,

Experience passion and power in six brand-new, provocative titles from Silhouette Desire this July!

Begin with *Scenes of Passion* (#1519) by *New York Times* bestselling author Suzanne Brockmann. In this scintillating love story, a pretend marriage turned all too real reveals the torrid emotions and secrets of a former bad-boy millionaire and his prim heiress.

DYNASTIES: THE BARONES continues in July with *Cinderella's Millionaire* (#1520) by Katherine Garbera, in which a pretty pastry cook's red-hot passion melts the defenses of a brooding Barone hero. *In Bed with the Enemy,* (#1521) by rising star Kathie DeNosky, is the second LONE STAR COUNTRY CLUB title in Desire. In this installment, a lady agent and her lone-wolf counterpart bump more than heads during an investigation into a gun-smuggling ring.

What would you do if you were *Expecting the Cowboy's Baby* (#1522)? Discover how a plain-Jane bookkeeper deals with this dilemma in this steamy love story, the second Silhouette Desire title by popular Harlequin Historicals author Charlene Sands. Then see how a brokenhearted rancher struggles to forgive the woman who betrayed him, in *Cherokee Dad* (#1523) by Sheri WhiteFeather. And in *The Gentrys: Cal* (#1524) by Linda Conrad, a wounded stock-car driver finds healing love in the arms of a sexy, mysterious nurse, and the Gentry siblings at last learn the truth about their parents' disappearance.

Beat the summer heat with these six new love stories from Silhouette Desire.

Enjoy!

Melissa Jeglinski
Senior Editor, Silhouette Desire

Please address questions and book requests to:
Silhouette Reader Service
U.S.: 3010 Walden Ave., P.O. Box 1325, Buffalo, NY 14269
Canadian: P.O. Box 609, Fort Erie, Ont. L2A 5X3

Expecting the Cowboy's Baby

CHARLENE SANDS

Silhouette

Desire

Published by Silhouette Books

America's Publisher of Contemporary Romance

SILHOUETTE BOOKS

ISBN 0-373-76522-3

EXPECTING THE COWBOY'S BABY

Visit Silhouette at www.eHarlequin.com

Printed in U.S.A.

Books by Charlene Sands

Silhouette Desire

The Heart of a Cowboy #1488
Expecting the Cowboy's Baby #1522

Harlequin Historicals

Lily Gets Her Man #554
Chase Wheeler's Woman #610
The Law and Kate Malone #646
Winning Jenna's Heart #662

CHARLENE SANDS

resides in Southern California with her husband, Don, and two children, Jason and Nikki. She's also the mother of two very spoiled cats, Skittles and Snickers, who basically rule the house. When not writing, she enjoys Pacific beaches, sitting down with a good book and, of course, happy endings!

She loves to hear from her readers. Contact her at charlenesands@hotmail.com or enter her contests at www.charlenesands.com.

To my author friends, who inspire,
support and encourage me each and every day.

To Tanya Hanson—
new author, friend and "drive" buddy.
I enjoy our times together.

To Debbie Decker—
who always has a smile and a kind word.
Your bubbly laughter is contagious!

To Barbara McCauley—
whose advice, help and friendship
is always appreciated.

To Sandra Madden—
my first and only real critique partner.
Wish you continued success.

And to the authors I hope to meet one day.
You got me hooked!
LaVyrle Spencer, Sandra Brown,
Janet Evanovich and Kathleen Woodiwiss.

One

Cassie Munroe raced down the hotel's hallway, her composure all but gone. A car breakdown on River Road miles away from your destination will do that to you, she supposed. Her Volkswagen Bug had run out of gas.

The last thing she wanted was to make a splashy entrance to her brother Brian's rehearsal dinner. Shamefully, she admitted she didn't want to make any sort of entrance. But she loved her brother dearly and wouldn't dream of missing his special day, even if she was out of work, out of a date for the wedding and almost out of time.

She searched the gold-embossed lettering on the doorways of the ballrooms as she strode past and found the room she'd been looking for. This had to be it. *Sunrise Room.*

Standing just outside, she straightened her clingy red dress, ran her fingers through her short hair and took a deep, steadying breath. Grasping the handle, she thrust the door open and entered. She was more than halfway through the room before she peered up and saw the banner.

Laughlin River Stampede Rodeo Banquet.

The big bold sign at the front of the room caught her off guard. She stopped in midstep and paused. A room full of cowboys, seated at a U-shaped table, all looked up.

Big, bold, Stetson-wearing, silver-buckled, *gorgeous* cowboys—all looking at her with interest.

The room quieted.

Cassie pasted on a smile.

Heavens, she'd never seen a better-looking group of men in her life. She made a mental calculation. Seventeen cowboys, she estimated, but this was not the time for her silly habit of counting everything that could be counted. Sometimes having a flair for numbers had its disadvantages.

"You're a bit early, honey. But don't think a soul's gonna mind," one of cowboys called. She would have dashed out of the room if he hadn't sounded so polite. "C'mon over here. We won't bite."

Male chuckles erupted all around.

Heat climbed up her neck. Suddenly, Cassie was aware of her attire. She'd wanted to look great today so she'd put on her most daring dress with a low-cut bodice and a hem riding high on her thighs. She'd slipped her feet into three-inch black stiletto heels and had her auburn hair highlighted and styled. Wasn't every day a girl had to face her ex-fiancé and his new bride.

At her brother's wedding, no less.

"Uh, no. Thank you," she countered, trying to be just as polite. "I think I have the wrong room. I'm supposed to be at a wedding rehearsal."

"Ah, now that's a doggone shame," the same voice cajoled. "I bet you want the Sunset Room, darlin'."

The Sunset Room? Yes, that was it. The dinner was to be held in the Sunset Room, not the Sun*rise* Room.

Running out of gas on that hot desert road must have addled her brain. She'd marched along that road, greatly intimidated by the dry brush and saguaro cactus surrounding her, hoping to find some relief. Finally, after walking what she'd estimated as a good long mile and a half, she'd come upon a roadside emergency phone. A tow truck driver with an attitude had rescued her just in time for her to make the rehearsal dinner. He'd given her grief for running out of gas in the desert and she'd endured his lecture all the way into town. Now, here she stood in the wrong room, facing a bunch of good-natured cowboys and probably looking just as foolish.

Cassie pivoted on her heels and headed straight for the exit and the Sunset Room.

A big, bold *handsome* cowboy blocked her way. How he got there, was a mystery. Seems she would have definitely noticed him when she walked in.

Number Eighteen was something to behold.

Lounging casually against the doorway, he gestured toward the front of the room with a slight tilt of his head. The Stetson he wore rode low on his forehead, casting his face in shadows, but Cassie noted strong features on an equally strong body. "You mean, you don't want to stay for the Meet and Greet?"

"The what?" Cassie asked, intrigued, more by the man than the question.

"Fans come to say hello, meet their favorite rodeo riders. We sign autographs, shake hands, take pictures. That sort of thing."

"Oh, so you're, uh…in the rodeo?" Silly question. Of course, the man was in the rodeo. Cassie had a thing for cowboys and could spot a real one a mile away. But all she'd met in Los Angeles over the past ten years was the proverbial "wannabe" cowboy. Men who dressed the part but probably had never mounted a horse in their life.

"Yes, ma'am."

"You don't ride bulls, do you?" Cassie was stalling. This cowboy was a great diversion; a sure way to keep from finding the "right" room and make a late *splashy* entrance to Brian and Alicia's dinner.

"Nope. I like to keep my body in one piece. I rope calves."

"I've never been to the rodeo, but if you don't mind me saying, roping calves sounds a bit cruel."

"Nah. Ain't a bit cruel. The calves we use are raised for it. Sort of like, it's their job." He reassured her with a quick smile, nudging his hat up higher on his forehead, giving Cassie a much better look at his features.

Uh-oh. Cassie blinked. Then blinked again. Her heart raced. Certain dread pulled at her. She recognized that smile, that handsome face. Years washed away in her mind and suddenly Cassie was a young teenage girl again, being stood up for the first time.

Jake Griffin.

Cassie stood frozen for a moment, taking note of the man he'd become. From the look of him, he'd done a great job of keeping his body intact. Yards of hard muscle lay underneath his Western shirt. And his sure enough attitude probably kept the ladies lining up. Heck, she'd been first in line years ago and look where that had gotten her.

Cassie couldn't believe her luck. Running into him today of all days! Wasn't it bad enough she had to endure the weekend in close proximity with her ex-fiancé, Rick? Now she had yet another brutal reminder of her lack of good judgment. Jake Griffin had been the first boy to disappoint her at the tender age of sixteen, leading to a world-class string of bad choices with the opposite sex. Cassie had a penchant for attracting troubled men. Jake had been the first—the lone wolf, the boy who didn't make friends easily and who seemed out of place, as though he didn't belong. She'd been drawn to him instantly and for a very short time in high school, she'd been his friend, hoping to become more.

Her brother Brian had always said she was too soft-hearted—a sweet marshmallow who would get squashed if she weren't careful. Her recent broken engagement to Rick had been proof positive that her older brother had been right. She'd been there for Rick when his life had taken a wrong turn. She'd comforted and consoled him, helping to bring him out of his emotional slump. And he'd honored her by a swift and effective betrayal.

Never again, Cassie vowed. She'd learned her lesson.

And she found the best way to solve her dilemma was not to give in to her attraction. Not to place any credence in her instincts. No more being suckered in by men who would steal her heart then walk away, pretty as you please. She had it all figured out in her head. All she had to do was get through this weekend and she'd be off and running. She'd be ready to start a new life.

Jake Griffin obviously didn't recognize her. It was a small consolation that did nothing for her ego. Get out fast, she told herself. "Uh, well, I'd better be going. Brian is going to worry himself sick, if I'm late."

A dark brow shot up. "Boyfriend?"

Cassie shook her head. "Brother. Now, if you'd please let me pass, I really have to get going."

He didn't budge for a second. Then when he removed himself from the doorway, he stared deep into her eyes. "Hate to let you go till I figure out how I know you."

Uh-oh. Cassie shot him an impatient glance. Women

probably never gave Jake Griffin that kind of look. Heck, if she wasn't dying to get away from him, praying that he wouldn't remember her, if she hadn't known him, she'd most likely stay and chat with the handsome calf roper. But she did know him and warning bells rang out loud and clear inside Cassie's head. Smartly, this time she listened. She brushed past him on her way out and smiled. "Nice try, cowboy."

Jake watched Miss Sexy Red Dress walk down the hall. The view from the back was just as appealing as the view from the front. That tight crimson dress hugged every curve the woman possessed, making the sight of her walking away pretty doggone awesome. But it was more than a dynamite body, soft auburn hair and silver-dollar-size green eyes that had drawn Jake to her.

He really felt that he'd met her before.

And then it hit him. He'd been thinking of the women he'd known in the present. But he'd known her as a girl— in the past. Another lifetime ago, it seemed.

"Cassandra Munroe," he called, stepping out into the foyer.

She halted, her shoulders slumping. She turned to him slowly. Those eyes, bright green and so incredibly startling, had given her away. No other female had eyes quite so remarkable. It had been years, ten or so, since he'd seen her. They'd only known each other for a short time while in high school and both of them had changed quite a bit, but Jake hadn't forgotten her.

He strode down the hallway, watching her indecision from the subtle moves she made. The tilt of her head feathered auburn tresses onto her cheek, the rest of her coppery hair shifting slightly. "You went to Santa Susana High School," he announced.

She stared at him a moment, her expression a mixture of emotions he couldn't read.

"Do you remember me?" he asked.

"Jake Griffin," she said, her tone flat. "We went to school together."

"Yeah, for about a minute." He removed his hat to scratch his head. "Hard kid to forget, huh?"

She stared at him a moment more with curiosity, it appeared, and a question on her lips. She fought a frown, but Jake noticed her struggle to keep her expression from faltering. "You look different," she said. "All grown up."

He cocked his head. "I could say the same about you, Cassandra." He couldn't pretend not to notice that Cassandra Munroe had grown up in very appealing ways. Her body was one to write home about and she had a unique face, not only those large, emerald eyes, but also a pouty, heart-shaped mouth and the prettiest silky hair.

"It's Cassie now." She darted a glance around, her eyes searching for the Sunset Room and a way out, no doubt. "I really am late. I should be going. It was nice seeing you again, Jake."

He doubted that. The woman's expression had chilled the minute he recognized her. Memories flooded in of his early high school days. Cassandra had befriended him when no one else had. He'd been a loner, an outcast, the boy even his biological father hadn't wanted. Jack Griffin had been the foster kid that nobody wanted. He'd been bounced around from one home to another. Six foster homes in all. At times, Jake knew he had no one to rely on but himself. He'd never stayed in one place long enough to make lasting friendships. He'd never developed roots of any kind. He knew for the most part, his foster parents hadn't cared for him. He'd been trouble at times. He hadn't been an easy kid to have around, and later, in his teens, he'd been the boy mothers warned their daughters about. Cassie probably should have steered clear, too, because in the end, he had only hurt her.

Jake reminded himself he was on a mission to win the rodeo championship. He had to prove to his estranged father once and for all that he was every bit the man that John T. was. It was a personal promise he'd made to himself. He had no time for red-haired beauties, anyway, old acquaintance or not. He had no time for women, period. He'd gone that route once before and it had ended with disastrous results. His wife had left him for a man with a more stable profession. She wasn't cut out to be a rodeo wife, she'd claimed, but Jake had known better. He'd known the truth— she'd abandoned him because she hadn't loved him enough, or at all. Jake had come to the conclusion, without a doubt, that he wasn't cut out for relationships, much less love.

He'd never known real love of any kind. It had been a long, hard road for a young boy, but he'd finally faced facts. Even his biological father hadn't wanted him, until John T.'s legitimate son had died tragically. Jake still had his doubts as to why John T. had finally come for him. But he'd vowed not to open his heart up to anyone, and that included his father. That also meant no women, no entanglements and no *distractions* of any kind. "Think you can find the Sunset Room?"

A small smile surfaced. "Don't worry about me. I'll be just fine."

Jake watched her walk away.

The woman certainly was "fine."

He shook his head and headed back to the banquet. A horde of fans pounced on him before he reached the door, jamming photos and programs in his hand for him to sign. But Jake had trouble concentrating on names being dashed off in rapid succession.

His mind was on one distracting female.

And he doubted he'd be able to forget the all-grown-up, Cassie Munroe anytime soon.

Brian hugged Cassie to his chest and kissed her forehead. He whispered, "Thanks for coming, sis. I know this isn't easy for you."

Cassie stared blankly at her brother, still reeling from seeing Jake Griffin again after all this time. He'd been a boy, a tall, good-looking one when she'd known him, but now…well, Jake was a hunk of a man with chiseled features, sexy stubble and a well-defined mouth. She'd had a major crush on him in high school and had been so darn giddy when the boy she'd only known for a few weeks had asked her out. And then, without reason, he'd broken her young, tender heart.

A sigh escaped Cassie's throat.

This weekend couldn't get any worse.

"Cassie?" Brian's voice brought her out of her musings. "Huh?"

"I said, I know this isn't easy for you."

No, it wasn't easy for her, but she'd made it through the rehearsal and now sat next to her brother, with Alicia by his side, in the Sunset Room and had to endure their sympathetic stares. They meant well, but Cassie was tired of being everyone's pity case. She'd made up her mind when Rick broke up with her that it was for the best. She'd just wished they'd have come to that conclusion before the wedding invitations had been sent out. But for Brian's sake, and for her own, she'd been very cordial about the breakup.

Rick Springer was Brian's friend and business partner. It wouldn't do anyone any good for Cassie to play the martyred soul. Cassie had come to Brian's wedding and had every intention of enjoying herself.

''When do we get to meet your date?'' Alicia's smile and hope-filled expression had Cassie's mind spinning. She couldn't let on that her date wasn't coming. True, a busted knee from playing basketball was a pretty good excuse, but Cassie was afraid that's exactly what it would sound like to Brian and Alicia. An excuse. And they'd start worrying about her again. That was the last thing Cassie wanted. And trying to figure out what to do about it during the five-hour drive here had distracted her. That's why she'd run out of gas. Nerves, and a mad dash to get here on time, had made mush of her brain.

Poor Alicia would be crushed to know Cassie was sans date for the wedding. Alicia had tried her best to be upbeat and had been a source of great comfort to Cassie when Rick had broken their engagement. She'd lent her support and had been a true friend.

Cassie braved a glance at her brother. Brian, too, waited patiently for Cassie's answer.

He'd been concerned about her, as well; had suggested many times to set her up with one of his clients since the breakup, but Cassie had always refused. She didn't need a dating service. Besides she knew almost all of Brian's clients, having worked on their accounting books. Cassie hadn't met anyone of interest in the small, personalized chain of sporting goods stores that Brian owned in Southern California.

Cassie took a bite of her chicken marsala, hoping for inspiration, and realized that she couldn't taste the food. Raw nerves apparently affected her taste buds, too. ''Um, he had an appointment he couldn't miss. He'll be here tomorrow for the wedding.''

Relief registered quickly on both of their faces and Cassie shot them a reassuring smile while she trembled inside.

Now what?

She'd have to make up another excuse tomorrow. She could only hope Brian and Alicia would be too caught up in their festivities to spend time worrying about her.

Or…she could find herself a date.

That would be a far better solution. She'd be able to save face, hold her head up high and she wouldn't hinder her brother's celebration.

Brian took hold of her hand and patted gently. "I hope you have a good time tomorrow. Alicia and I worried that coming to our wedding would be too soon for you."

"Oh, I'm fine. I'm over it, really, Brian. And I wouldn't dream of missing my brother's wedding. It's been three months and I'm…I'm actually glad I didn't marry Rick." She peered down the long table to the far end where Rick sat with his new wife. To her brother's credit, the newly married couple had been strategically placed as far away as possible from her. Mentally, she counted nine people separating them. Yet as she glanced at Rick, no emotion stirred within her, no regret or anguish.

After the breakup, Cassie had often wondered if Rick had been too darn convenient a choice. He was her brother's friend, business partner, someone Brian had approved of wholeheartedly. Had she considered marriage to Rick more for her brother's sake than hers? Cassie had never contemplated her motives with such scrutiny before. But she'd had time to really think in these last few weeks. And during that time she'd come to the conclusion that marrying him wouldn't have been the right move.

In truth, she wasn't going to marry anyone until she had her feet planted firmly on the ground. She wanted a fresh start and, surprisingly, she wanted small-town life again. She had wonderful fond memories of her northern Nevada hometown and had always longed to go back. When her parents passed on, she and Brian were shipped to Los Angeles to live with their aunt Sherry. Brian had taken to city life far better than Cassie. It seemed to energize him whereas Cassie found the big city draining.

After Aunt Sherry retired to Florida, Cassie stayed in Los Angeles mostly to be close to Brian, but she'd always missed the simpler side of life. She *needed* that, she mused, without question. Besides, she'd been under her brother's wing too long. She wanted to cut the apron strings and branch out on her own. As sweet as her older brother had been, worrying about her at each turn, lending his support, she had finally decided to make some changes in her life.

It was time for Cassie to take a stand.

She wouldn't tell Brian her plans to relocate until he got back from his honeymoon in Kuaui. She wouldn't tell him that she had a job offer in Nevada, very near her own hometown, and that all had been settled but the signing on the dotted line. Upon his return she'd explain to her brother how badly she needed to do this. She would make him see that she wasn't cut out for big city life.

"I can't wait to meet your date," Alicia said eagerly. Both she and Brian had looks of anticipation on their faces.

Cassie really hated lying. "He's just a friend, really. I mean to say, he's not my boyfriend or anything."

"He's coming all this way for our wedding. To be with you," Alicia reminded her.

Cassie's heart sunk to the floor. The soon-to-be married couple read far too much into this. And Cassie knew they only wanted her happiness. "Well, sure. But—"

"It's time for a toast," Rick said, rising from his seat with a glass held high.

All eyes at the table turned to Cassie, to see her reaction. It was natural for people to be curious, she supposed, but facing Rick and his new bride, after a humiliating breakup, was almost too much for her to bear. Yet she kept her composure and plastered on a smile for all to see.

For certain now, she had to find herself a date for the wedding. She couldn't take another day of concerned looks and sympathetic stares. There'd be no place to hide on the Sundance Riverboat Wedding Cruise tomorrow.

Unless she tossed herself overboard.

Two

Jake slipped into the back of the Caboose Lounge and took a seat at the hotel bar. It was Rodeo Days in the small river city and rodeo riders from all over the country were welcomed with open arms at the hotels. He ordered a straight-up whiskey and turned to listen to the Country Riders Band, hoping their down-home tunes combined with the shot of Wild Turkey would lull him into sleep mode. He'd been keyed up lately, too wired to sleep and anxious about the rodeo tomorrow. It was always the same. Nerves. Excess energy. When he knew he should be sleeping, his body never seemed to cooperate.

And visions of Cassie Munroe had danced in his head since he'd met up with her at the banquet today. He needed to get a grip, to get the tempting lady off of his mind and get some rest. What he didn't need was a distraction. He'd come so far and was extremely close to achieving a goal that had been just out of his reach for years.

Winning the rodeo championship meant more to him than the notoriety, money and respect he'd garner from his peers. Winning meant he'd done something that his father hadn't been able to accomplish. Winning meant he'd finally be able to look John T. in the eye and say that he was just as good a man, if not a better one.

He glanced at his watch. Damn, it was after midnight. He really should get some sleep. He ordered another drink, deciding to take it up to his room when a flash of red caught his eye. He stood up from his position on the bar stool and peered over the crowded room, thinking his mind played tricks on him.

But it was no trick of the mind. He *had* seen Miss Sexy Red Dress. He stepped in a bit closer, making his way forward, watching her move fluidly, her body gyrating like some exotic dancer's. Jake's chest tightened and when her cinnamon hair lifted then fell onto her flushed face, he cursed silently. Mesmerized, he continued watching her. Her green eyes, big, wide, animated, focused on the man she danced with.

Jake sat back in his seat and twisted his mouth in a frown.

The woman intrigued him, but better to take his drink up to his hotel room than to sit here and listen to his heart pound hard against his chest, watching her dance. Jake glanced back behind the bar. "Could you hurry it up?"

The young barkeep nodded his head. "Sure thing. Coming up in a minute."

When Jake turned around, another man held Cassie in his arms this time. This man he knew. Brody Taylor was a bull rider, full of himself and an all-around lady's man.

The music drifted into a slow, soulful ballad.

Jake stifled an oath when Brody brought Cassie up flush against his chest. He noted her squirming in his arms—or at least it appeared she was trying to break the connection.

None of his business, Jake thought, shaking his head. She'd given him the cold shoulder today once she'd realized who he really was. She didn't want him interfering in her life. He turned away to glance at the bartender again. His drink was nowhere in sight.

"You know what, forget it," he called to the bartender, who'd been flirting with some young blonde at the other end of the bar.

Jake stood, taking one last glance at the dance floor. He noticed Cassie slapping Brody's hands off her rear end. Fury exploded inside of him.

"Ah, hell," he muttered.

He made it to the dance floor in five quick strides and didn't bother tapping Brody on the shoulder. "I'm cutting in," he said firmly without giving Cassie a glance.

"Like hell you are." Brody turned, his body staggering some, his bloodshot eyes only just lighting with recognition.

"Time for bed, Taylor."

The bull rider slanted him a crooked, drunken grin. "That's what I'm aiming for, Griffin. Now get lost."

With a firm grasp, Jake removed Brody's arm from Cassie's. "Not with her, you're not." Jake pulled Brody's hat lower onto his head with a tug. "You got two bulls to ride tomorrow. If you don't get to bed soon, they'll knock you to Texas and back. Now, go on."

Brody hesitated for a moment, probably too drunk to argue, then nodded and tottered away, slurring curse words.

Jake finally peered at Cassie. She stood, somewhat dumbfounded, in the middle of the dance floor. "You okay?"

"Just fine," she said with definite irritation. That pretty heart-shaped mouth turned down into a pout. When Jake took her into his arms she asked, "What are you doing?"

"I'm cutting in. You do want to dance, don't you?"

She broke away from him. "No. Not anymore."

Okay, so she didn't want to dance with him. At least she wouldn't be fending off the likes of Brody Taylor into all hours of the night. He followed her when she walked over to her table. He hadn't noticed before, but she wobbled when she moved. And those bright, luminous eyes weren't so bright anymore. In fact, they appeared every bit as hazy as Brody's had been.

Cassie slumped down into her chair and took a big gulp from a fishbowl glass of margarita. He stood over her. "How many of those have you had?"

"Just one." Cassie looked up at him in defiance.

"One too many, I'd say."

Her lips quivered. She appeared so forlorn and her eyes misted with unshed tears.

"Hey, I didn't break something up back there, did I? If I did, I apologize. Want me to go hunt him down?" Hell, if she wanted Brody Taylor, she could have him. Jake wasn't going to break up a love affair, if that's what the woman was after.

"No, no. I don't care about him. I'm just…so tired. I took an allergy pill a while ago."

"And washed it down with the margarita?"

She nodded. "It's been a long day."

Cassie couldn't believe Jake Griffin was standing there, in the flesh. She'd been thinking about him all day. And the minute she'd laid eyes on him on the dance floor, her heart sped up and her toes curled. Just gazing up into his dark, ominous eyes made her dizzy. Well, the allergy pill had a little something to do with that, she assumed, but Jake Griffin was just too appealing. Cassie could never trust herself with him. She'd fall hard and then she'd shatter.

Besides, he was the last man on earth she should be thinking about. He'd been the first in a long string of bad decisions. The first one always hurt the most, she presumed,

because she'd been so trusting and it had been so unex-
pected. But the sad fact remained, Jake Griffin had stood
her up on what was to be her very first date ever, and the
sting of his betrayal wounded her like a gut-stabbing pain.
She'd cried the night away and had the worst weekend in
her young life. And now, he stood, with hands on hips,
looking better than ever, lecturing her on prudent drinking
habits.

"We both have things to do tomorrow. We should get
some sleep. Let me walk you to your room," he offered,
reaching for her hand.

Her *room?* Heaven help her! It just dawned on her that
she didn't have a room. She'd gotten back late this afternoon
with the tow truck, then made a spectacle of herself at the
rodeo banquet before she'd finally found the right room and
met with Brian and Alicia for their dinner. Immediately after
that, she'd dashed into the rest room, cleaned up a bit and
tried applying her hare-brained scheme of finding a date for
the wedding in this bar. She'd been here for three hours and
had completely forgotten to check in.

"I, uh...um. I don't have a room, exactly."

Jake lowered his head and searched her eyes. With a hint
of confusion he asked, "You don't have a room?"

"Yes, I do. I mean I have a reservation for a room, but
with all the commotion, I forgot to check in."

Jake ran a hand down his face. "Okay, come on. We'll
get you a room."

Cassie took his hand and stood up. Her head reeled and
the room spun out. She'd been too busy dancing to notice,
but once she'd sat down, everything seemed to hit her all
at once. "Uh...oh. I guess margaritas don't mix well with
antihistamines," she said, trying to keep her balance.

"Oh, man, Cassie. You're gonna have a whopper of a
headache tomorrow." He put his arm around her shoulder

and leaned her into him. They walked slowly toward the reservation desk and that was perfectly fine with her. Cassie liked being in Jake's arms. He felt solid and steady and he smelled so darn good.

No. No. Those were dangerous thoughts. Cassie's mind was too jumbled up to think clearly, but she did remember that Jake Griffin was off-limits. She could fall hard for her real-life cowboy. He'd hurt her in the past and would probably cause her pain again if she weren't careful.

When they reached the front desk, Jake swore. "Damn."

"What?"

She squinted at the reservation desk through hazy eyes, noting the place swarming with grumpy and beleaguered senior citizens. The chaotic line wrapped around the hotel lobby. Their loud rants rattled around in her head as they shouted out politically correct obscenities to anyone who would listen. Their bus had broken down in the desert. They'd missed their special dinner. They were hungry. They were tired.

Cassie's brain fuzzed out and her legs wobbled like Jell-O. "We're not waiting around," Jake stated plainly.

With a quick, efficient move, Jake swept her up into his arms. "You're bunking with me tonight."

Jake carried Cassie to the elevator. She weighed next to nothing, it seemed, and felt darn good in his arms. Little did he know this afternoon when he'd spotted her at the rodeo banquet that he'd be carrying Miss Sexy Red Dress up to his room tonight. Of course, not for the desired reasons, he thought with wry amusement. Even Jake had standards. He had a second bed in his room and that's exactly where he'd deposit her.

When Jake reached his floor, he headed for his room,

ignoring smirks and curious stares of the passersby in the hallway as they noted the woman out cold in his arms. She'd fallen into a druglike sleep the minute he'd entered the elevator.

With his keycard, he unlocked the door and, with a shoulder shove, pushed through the doorway. He uttered a curse, noting the dishevelment surrounding him. He'd thrown down his equipment on the bed in a hurry this afternoon.

Cassie stirred in his arms and he quieted her with soothing words. It would be better for both of them if she stayed asleep. Having her wake up in his room, in his bed, would be too great a temptation. With efficient thoroughness he removed as much equipment from the beds as possible. He tossed ropes, chaps, gloves and other gear onto the floor, then folded back the blankets on one of the beds. With care, he set Cassie down on her back. Immediately, she nuzzled her face into the pillow and sighed with undisguised pleasure.

That sigh unnerved him and heat surged through his body with rapid speed. Sweat broke out on his forehead and he quickly swiped at it, backing away from the gorgeous woman lying on his bed.

Get a grip, Jake. You can't get in bed with her. In fact, you'd better not touch her again tonight.

He was ready to cover her up with the blanket, but realized her shoes were still on. "Damn."

He went to the lower end of the bed and hesitated, glancing at the leggy woman in the red dress. The material had bunched way up, exposing firm, shapely thighs, legs that cried out for his attention. Jake heaved a heavy sigh and slowly lifted one shiny black heel off her foot, then the other, careful not to touch her in any other way.

Jake tossed her shoes aside, covered her up to her chin

and closed the drapes. In total darkness now, he might be able to forget that Cassie Munroe slept just three feet from him.

Cassie woke to the alluring aroma of fresh coffee. She opened one eye, then the other, and stared straight into the face of a cowboy. The man sitting on the opposite bed, dressed in Western gear, complete with a black Stetson, smiled. "Morning."

Cassie blinked, then blinked again. She wasn't dreaming. He was as real as Nevada heat and so was the hot mug of coffee sitting on the nightstand just inches from her face. She brought the covers up to her chin, probing her mind for answers. Slowly, and with great effort, she began to remember everything. Except how she got into this bed.

What happened last night…with Jake?

Heavens, it'd be just her luck to have a torrid night with the sexy cowboy and not remember a darn thing in the morning. "Morning…oh!" Her head and facial muscles ached. It actually hurt to talk.

"That bad?" he asked, sipping from his mug of coffee. "I would have let you sleep longer, but I didn't know what time your brother's wedding was."

Brian's wedding! Cassie bounded upright, then paid a heavy price for her quick move when her head spun. She slumped back down with a groan. "I have two questions. What time is it?"

"Ten-thirty."

That was doable. The wedding wasn't until later this afternoon. She had time for a quick makeover, hair and makeup after an abbreviated workout. She didn't have to be at the river dock until four-thirty.

"And…" she began, swallowing past a lump in her throat. This was a more difficult question. Fear ran rampant through her body in anticipation of the wrong answer. "And…well, um, what exactly happened last night?"

Slowly she sat up, bringing the covers with her. She peered directly into Jake's dark eyes.

"You sort of passed out."

That much she remembered. It was the "after" part that she couldn't recall. "I mean, between us, Jake?"

Jake rubbed the side of his nose and tried darn hard to conceal a grin. "Wish I could say I was unforgettable in bed, but guess not." He chuckled, then added, "Nothing happened, Cassie. When we couldn't get you a room last night, I brought you up here to sleep. And you *slept,* all night, in that bed, by yourself."

Cassie let out the breath she'd been holding. "Thank you," she said with great relief.

Jake sipped his coffee and eyed her. "Don't be so quick to thank me." A sinful smile graced his face. "I do have rules, like a woman has to be coherent when I make love to her."

Warmth spread to her cheeks and a deep flush of heat traveled the length of her. What an appealing thought, she mused, making love with Jake. Instinctively she knew he'd be great in bed.

Biting her lip, she looked away, taking in the Spanish motif of the room with its intricately carved dark wood furnishings and pictures of haciendas and vaqueros on the adobe walls. How fitting that she'd wake up in such a room with a cowboy. She turned to him again. "I'm really sorry about last night."

Jake removed his hat, tossing it on the bed. "Yeah, what was that all about, anyway?"

Cassie stared at the shiny black Stetson on the bed, imagining Jake wearing it and nothing else. The image flashing in her head brought hot tingles to her body. Cassie cleared her throat—and her mind. She *had* to get over her fascination with Jake Griffin. He was strictly off-limits.

"What was what all about?" She played dumb. She couldn't bear for Jake to know she was so desperate for a date to Brian's wedding that she'd actually set out to meet a man last night. Her plan had failed, and even if Jake hadn't intervened with that bull rider, she was doomed to disaster. Brody had already told her he wasn't sticking around after the rodeo. He had to head home, straightaway.

"Cassie, I doubt you're the type of woman who goes around picking up strange—"

"I'm not," she said in her defense. "I don't do that sort of thing. In fact, I've pretty much sworn off men for the rest of my life."

Jake cast her a dubious look then shook his head. "I don't understand."

No, he wouldn't understand. And she wouldn't tell him that she'd been a dismal failure with the opposite sex since the beginning of time, it seemed. Cassie didn't want to try anymore. She was through coming up with the short end of the stick. She'd drawn her last short straw. She wasn't going to play second fiddle again. To anyone.

Disheartened with the path her life had taken, she'd decided to take a stand. For once she was going to put her needs first. She had other things to focus on besides men…such as that promising new job she'd been offered. It was perfect. There wasn't even a need for her to find a place to live. All the arrangements had been made for her. The job was set. All she needed to do was to show up in three weeks and sign the deal.

"It's…complicated." She reached for the mug of coffee and took a long sip. The hot liquid slid down her throat like soft velvet, soothing her nerves and helping to clear her head. "Coffee is good," she said, gauging Jake's reaction to her obtuse answer.

He stared at her a moment, smiled, then jammed his hat onto his head. "Why don't you take a shower? I'll get your bags out of your car and you can change your clothes."

Cassie lowered the sheet a bit, noting that Jake had left her dress on last night. "Oh, yeah. I guess I'd better get going. I've got to check into my own room."

"Where are your keys?"

Cassie pointed to her purse. "In there. I think I'm on level three. Neon-yellow Volkswagen Bug."

"Don't worry, I'll find your car. How many of those bright yellow Bugs could there possibly be?"

Cassie chuckled, but her mirth was stymied when Jake tossed her one of his shirts. The one he'd worn last night. "Put this on after your shower. I'll be back later."

Cassie watched him rummage through her purse, come up with the keys and head out the door. As soon as he was gone she undressed quickly and, on impulse, donned his light blue chambray shirt. She closed her eyes and turned her face to the collar, inhaling deeply, taking in his spicy scent. "Mmm."

But then she snapped her eyes open instantly. She'd forgotten to give Jake the code to her car alarm. With the way things were going, hotel security might just arrest him for breaking and entering. She dashed to the door, took a step outside, catching sight of him at the elevators. "Jake!"

He didn't hear her.

She called again, stepping farther into the quiet hallway. "Jake!"

Finally spotting her, he cast her a questioning look. She waved him over and he left the elevators, heading back to his room. She met him just outside the doorway, gripping tight the shirt she wore. "Cassie?"

"I forgot to give you—"

"Cassie!" Brian's voice resonating in the hallway spelled out doom.

"Cassie!" Alicia's sweet voice coming from the same direction spelled out unabashed interest. Cassie didn't know which was worse. They approached her instantly, but both sets of eyes were on Jake.

Cassie wanted to melt into the floorboards. She wanted to wake up from this nightmarish dream. Neither was going to happen, so instead she looked her brother in the eye. "Good morning," she said cheerily.

Brian grunted. Alicia grinned.

Cassie knew what they were thinking. What else would they think seeing her dressed this way, just outside the hotel door, with handsome Jake Griffin standing by her side?

"What's going on?" Brian asked point-blank, staring straight into her eyes.

"Uh—"

"Oh, don't be silly, Brian. Your sister's a big girl," Alicia interrupted. "And this is her date, right?" Alicia smiled at her and continued. "Brian and I worried that you'd made up that whole story about having a date when he didn't show up with you for the rehearsal dinner. But it seems he made it here just in time for our wedding."

"In more than enough time," Brian said sourly, glancing at Jake then piercing her with a look. Things were spinning out of control and Cassie didn't have a clue how to put a stop to it.

"Well, aren't you going to introduce us?" Alicia asked, her eyes darting back and forth from Jake to her.

"Uh, of course." Brian had never met Jake before. Her brother had been away at college for most of Cassie's high school days. She put a hand on Jake's arm, giving him a little pleading squeeze. "Jake Griffin, I'd like you to meet my brother Brian and his fiancée, Alicia."

Jake shook hands with Brian. "Nice to meet you."

Brian nodded, then Alicia stepped up to give Jake a big hug. "I'm so glad to meet you."

"Nice meeting you, ma'am."

Alicia blinked and cast Cassie an approving look. "Oh, he's just precious, Cassie. Where did you two meet?"

Cassie hesitated, praying for divine guidance. "Uh, well, the truth is—"

Jake stepped closer, wrapping an arm around Cassie's waist. "Cassie and I go way back, don't we, honey?"

Cassie braved Jake a look, hoping to keep trepidation and fear out of her eyes. Yet she was grateful that he'd played along, for what it was worth. "Uh, yeah. Way back."

"Well, isn't that nice," Alicia said. "We'll want to hear all about that, later on. But right now I'm starving and Brian promised me a big breakfast, then it's off to the hairdresser. C'mon, Brian. Let's give these two some privacy. We'll see them at the wedding."

"Okay," Brian agreed. "We'll see you later, sis." He bent to give her a kiss on the cheek then said a brisk good-bye to Jake. Cassie watched the two of them head down the hallway.

When they were out of sight, Jake took hold of her hand and led her back inside the hotel room. "Mind telling me what that was all about?"

Jake stood with hands planted on his hips, staring at Cassie. She made her way to the bed and slumped down, biting her lip. He took a seat on the opposite bed, facing her, waiting. She wore his shirt, looked damned good in it, too, and her exposed legs were enough of a distraction to keep

Jake's mind from sorting all of this out on his own. He needed Cassie's explanation.

"This is embarrassing," she said, "and I'm sorry you got involved."

"Involved in what, Cassie?"

She looked into his eyes for a moment, then averted her gaze.

"Does this have something to do with that bull rider from last night?" Jake hoped not. For some bizarre reason, Jake's gut clenched at the idea that Cassie might be interested in Brody Taylor, in any way, shape or form.

"Sort of. I, um, needed a date for my brother's wedding. I, uh…oh, never mind. It's stupid." Cassie ran a hand down her face.

"Why is it so important that you have a date for your brother's wedding?"

Cassie crossed one leg over the other, a move that sped up his heart. She shifted on the bed, restlessly, and the shirt she wore—*his* shirt—moved fluidly with her, tempting him with a peek or two of her creamy skin above the knee. Jake curtailed his own desire to concentrate on what Cassie had to say. She stared into his eyes for a moment, then on a long sigh, began to explain. "Because, my ex-fiancé will be there with his new wife, that's why. Because the date I had for today isn't coming. And because I didn't want to face a crowd of people with pity in their eyes. It was bad enough yesterday at the rehearsal dinner when I showed up alone."

Jake twisted his lips. He was beginning to get the picture, although for all he was worth, he couldn't figure out why any man would dump Cassie Munroe. What had happened between them in high school didn't count, in his estimation. He hadn't dumped Cassie, but that night so long ago had been heart-wrenching for him and had changed his whole life. He couldn't explain that to Cassie. He never spoke of that night to anyone. But that didn't excuse the others who had treated her badly.

She was gorgeous in her own unique way and intriguing, if not a bit flighty. Those green eyes of hers could just about melt any man's heart. "I take it, it was a hard breakup?"

"Humiliating. Two days before the wedding. Then the guy turned around and married his tennis instructor, just two months later."

"That's rough," he said, understanding Cassie's dilemma better now. He leaned forward and took both of her hands in his, resting them on her thighs. He ignored the sensation ripping through him from that contact, the sharp pang of desire. He couldn't act upon his urges. Not now, not with Cassie so vulnerable. He wondered why she hadn't asked him to the wedding instead of trying to pick up some stranger. "You could have said something yesterday."

Stark fear entered her eyes and they went amazingly wide. "Oh, I couldn't ask you. You're the last man I'd ask."

Jake flinched, his body tightening. The sting of her pronouncement ran deep, cutting through his heart. He'd been the outcast in school, the foster kid nobody seemed to want. And later he'd been the bastard son of a cold unyielding man. His own father hadn't wanted him until it was too late. Far too late. Jake had known rejection all of his life. He'd dealt with it in his own way. Somehow it always managed to hurt, though, even when it came from a woman he'd just barely met. He dropped her hands and sat back, wondering how many times he'd have to feel this way. How many more times would the pain of rejection slash through his gut? Hell, he'd given up the battle years ago when Lorie had deserted him, but dammit, he wanted to know why Cassie wouldn't even consider him. Or had that one night in high school, when he hadn't showed, been that devastating to her? "Because of what happened in high school?"

Cassie closed her eyes briefly, as though reliving that night, then cast him a somber glare. "Being stood up for homecoming is a pretty big deal for a young girl."

A tick worked at Jake's jaw. "I know. But it had nothing to do with you."

"It was as if you'd just dropped off the planet, Jake. I never heard from you again."

Jake gritted his teeth. Just when life should have been about cars and girls and going out with your friends, his life had been a mess. And he had pretty much dropped off the planet. His father had finally admitted Jake's existence that night and had come for him. In one insane instant Jake's whole life had changed. "It couldn't be helped, Cassie." Jake paused. "Is that the only reason you don't want me taking you to the wedding?"

"Not exactly," Cassie answered. "I have a much better reason."

Jake couldn't wait to hear this one. "I'm listening."

She looked him dead in the eyes, hers, wide, green and so honest. "It's because I'm attracted to you."

Jake flinched again. He took a moment to let that sink in, staring at her, trying to understand what the woman meant, but none of it made sense. It was the last thing he'd expected her to say. "And that's a bad thing?"

She bobbed her head up and down. "Oh, a very bad thing. You see, I'm a terrible judge of what's good for me. What happened in high school with you was just the beginning. From then on I made a string of bad choices, always hooking up with the wrong guy. I've been hurt, Jake, and I don't trust my instincts anymore. I've made too many mistakes. I refuse to make any more. That's why that bull rider would have been perfect for me. I didn't feel a thing for him.''

Jake silently applauded her for that. He slid his hand down his jaw and took a deep breath. Leaning toward her again, he took her hands in his, greatly relieved her rejection hadn't been entirely because of him or that one night, but because of her own insecurities. He owed this woman and a compelling tug in his heart had him offering to help her. ''Listen, Cassie, I'd be lying if I said I wasn't attracted to you, too. That's not the issue here. Besides, tomorrow we're both going our own separate ways, right?''

Cassie nodded slowly, keeping her gaze fastened to his.

''Let me take you to your brother's wedding. It'd be like a make up date for the one in our past. We'll spend the evening together. You'll be able to enjoy the wedding and then we'll part company. It's as simple as that.''

''I don't know.'' She began shaking her head. Jake knew she didn't really trust him. He couldn't blame her for that. They really didn't know each other anymore. All she had to go on was what she knew of him in the past. And he hadn't left her with a good impression. But Jake felt a compelling need to set this one part of his past to rights.

He couldn't afford anything more with Cassie Munroe.

''Look, your brother already thinks I'm your date. Why change that?''

Cassie hesitated, drawing in her lower lip, contemplating. Finally she asked, ''You really think we can pull it off?''

Jake nodded. ''We can manage one evening together, don't you think? We've already spent a night together, and that didn't turn out so badly, did it?''

She chuckled, the sound a relief to his ears. ''No, not really.''

''What time is the wedding?''

''We have to be at the riverboat dock at four-thirty.

They're getting married under the London Bridge in Lake Havasu, so the boat has to leave on time."

Jake calculated his timetable. "I've got a rodeo event scheduled today. I have to compete. I need those points to win the championship. It's been my goal for five years and this is the closest I've come. But I'll meet you at that dock at four-thirty. It's a promise."

Cassie stood and for the first time today she appeared hopeful. "Okay, that's the best offer I've had in months. I'd better get into the shower then."

He rose from the bed, also. "I'll get your bags out of the car. Just give me the code this time, okay?"

"Okay, and thanks, Jake." Cassie stood on tiptoes and brought her lips to his, ready to give him a quick kiss.

On instinct Jake cupped her head, feeling the silkiness of her short hair fall through his fingers. He bent her head up and brought his mouth down, taking a full taste from her lips. She was sweet and giving and her mouth moved with his too well. She made a little whimpering sound that sped his pulse and he deepened the kiss, pressing her closer, realizing that their bodies touched intimately. Jake backed up slightly, holding her away, fearful she'd know the true extent of his desire. He wanted her. But he wasn't going to do a darn thing about it.

He was righting a past wrong, doing them each a favor, and then they'd part company, just as he'd pledged.

Three

Cassie stood on the boat dock, looking out at the bright blue water of the Colorado River rushing by. Its quick, unyielding flow matched the pace of her heartbeats. With clear skies and a slight breeze, it was the perfect setting for a wedding on a riverboat.

She clutched her black satin purse tight and glanced at her watch, realizing that it was already past four-thirty. Many of the passengers had already boarded, the captain ushering them on with a graceful smile. Cassie closed her eyes and held her breath, taking in warm Nevada air. Any minute now she'd have to board that boat, alone.

No use prolonging the inevitable, she thought. Jake wasn't a man to be trusted. He'd told her what she wanted to hear at the moment, but he hadn't followed through. She'd been a fool, once again where Jake Griffin was concerned. Now she had to face Brian's guests and her ex-fiancé Rick included, alone. So be it. Cassie mustered her courage, fighting off disappointment, and began the lonely climb across the plank leading to the *Sundance.*

Darn, she'd been looking forward to having Jake accompany her to the wedding, but maybe, in the long run, this was for the best. After the way he had kissed her this morning in the hotel room, Cassie's mind went on a downward slide. No man had ever kissed her with such immediate urgency and passion. No man had ever made her knees buckle like that before. And no man wore a Stetson the way Jake Griffin did.

All the more reason she should be glad he hadn't made it on board.

Cassie strode along the lower deck of the boat, smiling at Brian and Alicia's guests as she approached the crowded cocktail bar. She ordered a drink and waited patiently. She had nothing but time. The wedding ceremony wouldn't happen for at least an hour. When the boat began to move away from the dock, she sighed with resignation.

Just a few more hours, Cassie, and it will all be over.

"Whiskey sour, for the lady," the bartender said with a sly wink, sliding the glass her way.

"Thanks." She picked up her drink, brought the glass to her lips and was ready to take a sip when the drink was gently removed from her hands.

"Don't think so, Cassie."

The deep, silky sound of Jake's voice made her breath catch. Her heart did little joyful flips and shivers of delight carried throughout her body. He'd made it on board. "Jake?"

She turned and was immediately thunderstruck by his appearance. He was dressed in black, from head to toe, starting with that shiny black Stetson she'd had fantasies about, a dark Western suit and newly polished snakeskin boots.

"In the flesh," he answered, downing her whiskey sour in one giant gulp. "There, less temptation for you."

She swallowed, noting that *he* was all the temptation she could manage tonight. "I—I was sure you changed your mind."

"Nope, just got behind schedule. Rodeo didn't start on time."

"Did you win?" she asked, relief at having a date for tonight mingling with her fear at having a date for tonight. At having Jake as her date for tonight. Jeez, it was a definite catch-22 situation. But he was here now, and Cassie had to keep her head. They'd have a pleasant evening, then part ways. Jake hadn't offered anything else, so she shouldn't be worried. They could pull off one night together.

But heavens, the man sure cleaned up nicely.

"Yep. I won." He grinned, a charming lifting of lips that had Cassie remembering how good his kisses were. "I'm in the finals for tomorrow. You said you've never been to the rodeo. Why don't you come?"

"Oh, I couldn't. I'm leaving for L.A. first thing in the morning."

He shrugged. "If you change your mind, I'll leave a pass for you at the gate. Starts at twelve noon."

"Thanks, Jake. And thanks for coming today."

He nodded. "You look gorgeous," he said, and from the appreciative gleam in his eyes Cassie knew it wasn't just a line. Jake had a way of looking at her that made her feel soft and feminine. At least the two hundred dollars she had spent on the black satin cocktail dress hadn't been for nothing. Jake seemed to like it on her just fine. "Just promise me, no more hard liquor. Your head must have just settled."

Cassie laughed. "Well, yes. The throbbing did simmer down about an hour ago. I guess I wasn't thinking when I ordered that drink."

And she was barely able to think straight now, having Jake standing so close. He took her hand. ''Come on, Cassie. Let's take us a little stroll on deck.''

Holding hands with Jake had the desired effect. The same people who'd given her sympathetic stares not twenty-four hours ago were now casting her appreciative nods. It shouldn't matter. It shouldn't be so all-fired important. And perhaps it wouldn't have been so bad if the man who had jilted her hadn't been attending the celebration with his new wife. Cassie could have managed Brian's wedding otherwise. And Cassie admitted to herself, Jake Griffin was a boost to her ego, even if this whole evening was a sham. He was drop-dead gorgeous, likable and dangerous enough to keep her on her toes. For tonight at least, she'd enjoy having him be her pretend date.

Jake stopped by the railing and, pulling her close enough to brush hips, whispered in her ear, ''That's your ex over there, isn't it?''

With a slow turn of her head, Cassie spotted Rick with his wife by the bow of the boat. ''Yes, how'd you know?''

Jake turned to her, looked into her eyes then bent his head. When he lowered his mouth to hers, Cassie knew he was about to kiss her. A thrilling sensation caught her completely off guard. She put thoughts of Rick, the wedding, the boat—everything—out of her head. Jake's lips met hers, drawing deep from the contours of her mouth. He wrapped his arms around her waist and she moved into him until their bodies meshed.

The impact stunned her. His nearness. His sexy scent, made up of musk and man. When the brim of his Stetson brushed her head, her legs wobbled and her heart raced with each moment that passed. Being in Jake's arms did astonishing things to her. She shouldn't indulge in such pleasurable, exciting, risky things, yet she hadn't the power to stop it.

Jake broke off the kiss, leaving her trembling. "He hasn't taken his eyes off you. I saw him darting glances when his wife wasn't looking. Thought we'd give him something worth watching."

"What? Oh, you mean, Rick?" All was suddenly clear. The kiss was meant for Rick to witness. Jake was playing the part of boyfriend, kissing her in front of the man who'd dumped her, making sure he'd taken a good hard look. It was a sweet gesture but Cassie's stomach churned bitterly at the deceit. Secretly she'd hoped Jake had kissed her for other reasons, none of them having to do with showing up her ex-fiancé.

"Yes, we gave him something look at," Cassie agreed quietly. She turned to gaze out at the scenery passing by. White water vanished into blue as the paddle wheel spun around and around, not entirely unlike Cassie's head at the moment.

An hour later Cassie dried her tears with a wipe of her hankie. Brian had just spoken his vows to Alicia and two had become one on a crystal-blue lake under an ancient, elegant bridge. Jake stood by her side, and when he glanced down at her teary face, he cast her a quick smile and took hold of her hand, entwining her fingers with his. The gentle pressure he applied to her hand was meant to reassure, but it had a different effect entirely. Tingles surfaced, a common occurrence she'd come to know when making contact with Jake, and every nerve in her body was fully, completely aware of the hunky cowboy.

Cassie warned herself not to indulge in her fantasy.

She had to come to grips with reality—Jake was doing her a favor. The wedding was probably the last place he'd choose to be right now. He was a rodeo rider, focused on winning the championship. He had places to go, people to see, a man without roots, it seemed. She'd better remember that her wild attraction to him would be fruitless and a big mistake. She'd witnessed passion in his eyes when speaking of his life with the rodeo. She'd sensed his drive and something underlying on his expression, something guarded, something he kept hidden. Perhaps there was more to his great ambition to win the championship than he would allow a stranger.

After the ceremony Jake led her over to the newlyweds in the reception area, where she hugged Alicia with great affection and kissed her brother's cheek. "It was a beautiful ceremony. I wish you both all the happiness you deserve."

Jake shook Brian's hand and kissed Alicia's cheek. "Congratulations."

"I'm so glad you made it to the wedding, Jake," Alicia said, smiling.

"Jake is with the rodeo, Alicia. He had a competition today and made it just in time," Cassie offered in explanation.

"Oh, then the captain must be a fan of yours. He said he wouldn't leave the dock until a very important guest arrived. I take it, that was you, Jake?" Alicia asked, her curiosity written all over her face.

Jake cleared his throat, darting her a glance. "I guess so. Lucky for me, he didn't shove off right on time."

Brian leaned in to kiss Alicia's cheek. "The music is starting up. It's time for me to take my new wife for a spin on the dance floor. They're playing our song, sweetheart."

Cassie watched Brian whisk his bride away. They stepped onto the small parquet dance floor as a five-piece band began to play. After the first song the bandleader welcomed all other couples to join in.

"Well?" Jake asked, a crooked smile gracing his mouth.

"You wouldn't dance with me last night. How about it? Want to dance now?"

He ran his hands up and down her arms; a brief touching that heated her skin instantly. Inwardly she flinched at the raw power he had over her, the way a single touch could make her come alive. She gazed into a set of dark, appealing eyes and knew she should refuse. Jake had been by her side all afternoon, touching her at every turn, creating more heat inside her body than a fiery furnace. He'd been attentive, aware of curious eyes and playing the game, but Cassie had begun to enjoy his attention a little too much. He almost made her forget that this wasn't real. He'd be leaving after the rodeo tomorrow and she'd return to Los Angeles. They'd head off in different directions and never see each other again.

"I'd love to dance with you," she blurted.

His grin reminded her of a swashbuckling pirate, of a handsome rogue, but most of all, that particular lifting of his lips reminded her of a devilish outlaw ready to ride into the sunset with the girl.

He lay a possessive hand to the small of her back and led her onto the dance floor. "I don't remember you asking me to dance last night," she said as he took her into his arms. She'd better keep a conversation going, she thought, or she'd get too wrapped up in the soft music, the sway of their bodies and the solid, warm feel of him.

"Doesn't surprise me. You weren't thinking too clearly yesterday." There was a note of irritation in his tone.

Cassie pursed her lips. "What do you mean by that?"

"I mean," he said, loosening his hold on her to gaze directly into her eyes. "Brody Taylor would've been your worst kind of nightmare, Cassie. I couldn't stand there another second and watch him manhandle you."

Cassie lifted her chin with defiance. "I don't recall any manhandling."

Jake pulled her in close with a strong tug, causing the air in her lungs to swoosh out. She fell against the solid wall of his chest, her breasts crushing into him. A little groan escaped his throat. He sucked in oxygen then continued. "Exactly my point."

Cassie didn't want a lecture from Jake. She didn't need to be reprimanded. She'd done what she'd had to do last night and only by the grace of good fortune had things worked out in her favor today. Well, she mused, that still remained to be seen. If Jake was going to bully her, then neither of them was going to have a good time tonight. "Nothing would have happened with him, Jake. I knew enough to keep my head, achy as it was."

"How can you be so sure?"

Why did he care? They'd only just met and he acted as though they were a real couple. From his tone he seemed to be more than a little curious about her answer. Had he been jealous of Brody?

"Because, Mister-Know-It-All Cowboy, I told you before, I didn't find him the least bit attractive."

"Rii-iight," he replied with a twist of his mouth. "The perfect guy for you. Someone who doesn't make your hair curl."

He made her hair curl, and her toes and her stomach. Darn him. Why did she have to find *him* so attractive?

"And I don't claim to know it all, but I do know what's on a man's mind when he's holding a beautiful woman in his arms."

He thought she was beautiful. Cassie's heart fluttered.

"Care sharing those insights with me?"

He shook his head. "Not a chance, honey."

"Doesn't matter. I'm not looking for anyone, anyway. I'm through with men."

"Uh-huh."

And if he were the type, he would have rolled his eyes, but Cassie heard disbelief in his tone. "You don't believe me?"

"Nope. You've got too much going for you to live the rest of your life alone. You're hurting right now, but you'll heal. And then some lucky guy will hog-tie you to him."

She stopped dancing to make her point. "I'm over the hurt, Jake. I need…space and freedom. I've never had that before. Brian's been wonderful to me, but he's overprotective. He's made my life too easy. He's been accommodating and I've allowed it. I think that's why I've made so many errors in judgment lately. It's my own fault for not being stronger. But now, well…things are about to change."

"Are they?"

"Yes, they are," she replied firmly.

"How?"

"I'm giving up my position at Brian's company. I've accepted a job near my hometown that I'm very excited about. I'm through with the big city. I haven't told Brian yet, so please don't mention it. I don't want my older brother to go into cardiac arrest anytime soon, especially right before his honeymoon."

"What do you do, exactly?"

"I'm an accountant. I've always been good with numbers. I'm forever calculating things in my head. It's almost an obsession."

He stopped to gaze at her. He spoke softly with an appreciative gleam in his eyes. "You don't look like an accountant."

"I, uh…is that a compliment?"

Jake chuckled. "Yes, ma'am."

"And to set the record straight," she added, "the last thing I want is to have some Neanderthal hog-tie me to him."

"If you say so," he said a little too smugly. Heck, what did she care if he didn't believe her? It wasn't as though they meant anything to each other. They were reunited acquaintances who would soon say their farewells tonight, and that would be that.

Jake must have been on the same wavelength, because the conversation died and he brought her up close again, pressing her to his solid body.

They moved fluidly across the dance floor, Cassie falling into step with him. He draped his hand down her lower back, dangerously near her derriere, while the other hand played with the ends of her hair. His warm breath caressed her lightly as he nuzzled his nose into her neck, breathing her in, creating exciting thrills throughout her body.

His hand slipped farther down her back, nearly *not* on her back any longer, and he whispered into her ear, "You're a beautiful woman, Cassie Munroe."

"Thank you. You're not half bad, yourself." It was an understatement by any stretch of the imagination. The man was sexy, thrilling, dangerous and...beautiful.

"Now that's nice to hear," he said in a husky voice, leaning in, bending to her. His lips traveled along her throat, moistening, kissing, nuzzling until Cassie couldn't take a deep breath. Her heart raced wildly. She kept telling herself it was all for show. Rick and his wife were on the dance floor, too. Jake must have noticed them. He was doing this for their benefit, not because he couldn't keep his hands off of her.

Those warning bells in her head rang loud and clear. *Don't fall for this guy. He's all wrong for you.*

Cassie reminded herself Jake was the first guy ever to

stand her up. And he hadn't offered her any explanation. Even though it happened more than ten years ago, a girl had a right to know why.

Cassie was eventually saved by the bell…the dinner bell. The band stopped playing and all the guests headed for the dinner tables, situated both inside and outside on one of the three-tiered decks.

It was a good thing, too, that dinner had been called, because Cassie needed to get a grip. Grateful that Jake opted for outdoor dining, they sat at a little table for two on the lower deck of the riverboat. Cassie needed the fresh air. She needed to clear her head. She needed to have a table separating the two of them or else she'd surely experience a meltdown.

She concentrated on the meal set in front her and when the waiter offered her a glass of Chardonnay, she didn't refuse. She took a bite of her New York steak, picked at the small potatoes and played with her salad.

"Not hungry?" Jake asked, watching her intently, those dark eyes considering her every move.

She sipped from her wine again and shook her head. "I guess I lost my appetite."

But it was obvious Jake hadn't. He'd finished his meal and was polishing off another glass of wine.

He stood and took her hand. "Come on. Let's take a walk."

As they strolled along the deck, Jake wrapped an arm around her shoulders, bringing her in close. They moved along slowly, like two rapt lovers enjoying time together. He played the part well, she thought. No one would ever believe they'd only met yesterday when she'd crashed the rodeo shindig.

Cassie gazed out as sunlight cast its last stunning glow on the water, a sheen that coated the surface with such brilliance that she had to squint slightly to take in the view. She let out a contented sigh. "Oh, this is lovely."

Jake stopped and turned her into his arms. Cassie gazed up into his eyes, the dark gleam perusing her intently. "It surely is," he said softly.

His hands found her waist and he pulled her in, pressing their bodies together. She took breath from her lungs, deep, soulful-steadying breaths, hoping to keep her balance, to keep from falling, but it wasn't working. Not with the way Jake Griffin was looking at her.

He cocked his head and kissed her again, this time with more heat, more passion than before. Parting her lips, he teased her with the tip of his tongue. The sensations whirling inside her stomach made her ache with need. She whimpered when his tongue took full possession and was gratified to hear him let out a groan of pleasure.

He tasted like wine. He smelled of musk. He felt so solid. Cassie's mind shut down. She was going on instincts now, those darn, pesky instincts she didn't trust. But she gave in to Jake, to the power of his kiss, the press of his body, completely consumed by uncontrollable desire.

"Jake?" she said finally, pulling away from him. She was about to ask him what was happening between them. She was about to ask him what it all meant, this wild, crazy passion they shared, but then she heard a familiar voice and turned slightly to find Rick standing just a few feet away with his wife.

Fool. Fool. Fool.

Cassie berated herself mentally over and over for thinking that Jake might not have been pretending. That maybe he'd experienced the same overpowering urges she had on the dance floor, during dinner and on the deck right now.

It had all been for show. She knew that now. Jake, making up for the date he felt he owed her, was doing his best to play the part of attentive boyfriend. And she'd been fool-ish enough to read more into it than that. Jake was no slouch in the kissing department. He probably didn't know how to kiss a woman any differently. And she'd fallen for it, hook, line and sinker.

Proof positive her instincts were out of whack.

Jake looked deep into her eyes. "Cassie? What is it?"

Cassie struggled for an answer, a witty retort, something to keep Jake from looking at her with those searching, as-sessing, knowing eyes. "W-what time is it?"

Jake blinked. "You want to know the time?"

She bit her lip then nodded.

He glanced at his watch. "It's just eight."

"That late? I have to get inside. I'm giving Brian and Alicia a toast before they cut the cake."

Eight o'clock, Cassie thought with newfound hope. Just another hour or two and they'd be off this boat then she would be done with this pretense and forget she'd ever laid eyes on Jake Griffin.

Jake helped Cassie step down from the *Sundance* onto the riverboat dock. He took hold of her hand, entwining his fingers with hers, needing the connection of her small hand in his. He held on tight, realizing his time with her was limited.

Jake had never been so drawn to a woman before. He'd done his best to steer clear tonight, but had wound up hold-ing her every chance he could and kissing her more times than was wise. She was soft and sexy, a knockout in black satin, yet her big, luminous eyes spoke of vulnerability, of disappointment and heartache. That, more than her striking appearance, seemed to draw him to her. He'd known some-thing of disappointment in his life and knew the signs all too well. Perhaps it was the reason he couldn't seem to take his eyes off her, couldn't quite manage to keep his hands to himself and couldn't help fantasizing about making love to her and wondering what it would be like.

In a few minutes he'd take her up to her hotel and say a polite farewell. He'd deposit her safely in her room, having helped her get through her brother's wedding tonight without humiliation, his self-proclaimed debt to her paid.

For Jake, it was the only way.

She didn't fit into his plans.

She never would.

They walked quietly on the Riverwalk, a lengthy sidewalk that ran alongside the river, with streaming moonlight as their guide. The beauty of the night seemed to be lost on Cassie. Deep in thought, she spoke little as they made their way into the hotel lobby.

Once inside the elevator, Cassie leaned heavily against the wall, gave him a smile that seemed a bit too cheerful for her mood, then closed her eyes. The tiny satin purse she carried dropped from her hand.

"I'll get that," he said, bending to retrieve the purse, but the view from down there put a lump in his throat. Those shiny black heels seemed to mock him and her lean, shapely legs, slightly bent at the knee, had him swallowing hard. He stood and draped the purse over her shoulder, but made the mistake of gazing into Cassie's large, green, beckoning eyes.

When she looked up at him like that, he lost all semblance of control. His groan echoed in the small elevator and as soon as the elevator stopped and the doors opened, Jake grabbed Cassie's hand and tugged her along the hallway until they finally reached her hotel room door. "Jake, what's the rush?" she asked.

"No rush," he lied, trying desperately to slow his heart down. If he didn't say good-night to her now, quickly, no telling what might happen. Struggling for composure, Jake lifted the corners of his mouth, attempting a smile. "You made it through the wedding pretty darn good."

Her deep sigh pressed black satin material even tighter against her chest, the neckline revealing more creamy skin than Jake could handle at the moment. "Thanks to you. You saved the day, Jake. Maybe you're my white knight."

He grunted and ignored her statement. "I guess this is good night and goodbye."

Cassie put her head down, studying the floor for a moment, then with a tilt of her head she met his eyes. She peered at him with gratitude written all over her face. "I'll never forget what you did tonight. You played your part so well, I think everyone was convinced you were my boyfriend." She shook her head, her luminous eyes filled with awe, but he witnessed more in those eyes, a hint of regret and anguish. "You must have a sixth sense or something, you always seemed to know when Rick was around." She appeared to shake off that thought with a toss of her head. "Anyway, thank you for what you did, and good luck with winning the championship." She put out her hand.

Her hand?

Jake stared at her small hand, which fit so perfectly in his. After a long moment he finally took it, squeezing gently. "Have a safe trip home, Cassie Munroe."

She bit down on her lip and nodded, staring at him with those incredible eyes. Deep, soulful emotions were wrapped up in her gaze and Jake saw them all; unguarded, exposed, heartfelt emotions. War raged inside his head, but he knew he'd lose the battle if he stayed a moment longer. He turned away from her and walked down the hallway. When he heard the soft click of her door, his gut clenched as though he'd been sucker punched.

Damn.

He turned on his heel, a quick pivot that brought him back to her door in three long strides. He'd let her believe too many untruths tonight, for his own peace of mind, but it wasn't fair to Cassie. She didn't have faith in herself or trust her instincts anymore. She didn't have confidence in her womanhood.

She didn't know she could knock a man to his knees with just a look or a slight toss of her hair. She didn't know her own appeal, having been with the wrong men—men who didn't appreciate her. She talked a good game, wanting independence from her overprotective brother, yet her eyes spoke of vulnerability, a deep struggle to keep afloat in her world of bad decisions. He had to set it all to rights.

Jake knocked softly on her door. "Cassie."

The door opened slowly and she gazed up with those big, incredible, emerald eyes. The overpowering effect she had on him brought a silent curse to his lips. "I ride a horse, Cassie, but I'm no white knight. And I wasn't pretending tonight, about anything. You got that? I saw your ex once, on the deck when I kissed you. If he was around after that, I didn't notice because I was too darn busy noticing you. It was all I could do to keep my hands off you. I'll admit I didn't do a very good job of that. You're a beautiful, sexy woman and I wish like hell—"

"Oh, Jake," Cassie said on a gasp, her eyes misting with tears. "I'm wishing, too."

He reached for her, pulling her close, and she came apart in his arms, falling into his embrace, her head tucking under his chin. The small iota of willpower Jake had left vanished like dust in a windstorm. Holding her in his arms stirred up all manner of emotion Jake usually kept locked away.

"Cassie," he uttered urgently before lifting her face to his and taking her mouth in a burning kiss. She tasted sweet, a hint of heady wine and willing woman, so uniquely Cassie. And the little throaty moans she made, of pleasure and desire, tossed him straight over the edge. Heat swamped him and the profound effect she had on him shred any semblance of sensible thought. He pressed his body against hers, showing her what he wanted, granting her the only part of him he had to give. ''I've got nothing to offer you,'' he breathed softly, ''but tonight.''

Four

Sold, Cassie thought.

She'd take Jake Griffin, even if it was just for one night. She knew they had no future, their paths and dreams too far apart to ever collide again, but Cassie couldn't think beyond the impact of Jake's fiery kisses, the overpowering heat his touch created, the solid strength of his body against hers. Cassie knew as soon as he'd closed the door behind them, her fate was sealed.

She moved with him, backing up toward the bed as he drove her wild with undisguised passion. His lips mastered her mouth and his hands finessed her curves, while his body heat coaxed her into oblivion.

He drove his tongue in her mouth, applying sweet, unyielding pressure, the impact of his kiss pulling her closer, melding them together as their bodies touched wildly, intimately, chest to chest, hip to hip, thigh to thigh. Cassie moaned softly, the sound escaping her throat with unabashed pleasure. She'd never known heat like this before, the flame within her body burning bright and hot. All of her senses were fine-tuned. She heard every sound, envisioned every move, felt every single nuance that was Jake.

She kissed him freely, openly, holding nothing of herself back. And when he groaned deep and low into her mouth, she knew instinctively what that meant. Jake, hot and hard, was ready. His erection pressed against her like steel and Cassie was in awe, anxious for him to take her.

In a flurry, clothes were tossed off, leaving a trail of garments on the floor. There was no time to think beyond the thrilling sensations whirling through her body like wildfire. Cassie burned with need, a blaze that only Jake could extinguish. She lay on the bed and he followed her. The sheer masculine strength of him, his massive chest, perfectly sculpted, called for her touch. She lifted a hand to graze his hot skin and he groaned again. "Damn...Cassie."

He traveled kisses from her mouth, down her throat and lower to the swell of her breasts. His lips hovered there, moistening her with his tongue, paying homage and creating magic with sweet, crushing caresses. Cassie's body ached with anguished need, the torture Jake created could only find one release. She arched up, little sounds of pleasure escaping her throat, wanting him to take more, to have it all.

Threading her fingers through his hair, Cassie closed her eyes, relishing the heat, the sensations and the breathtaking splendor of being with Jake. And when his hand moved lower, skimming her torso and lower yet, teasing, tempting, until finally he met the need Cassie silently demanded, she arched up even higher to take what Jake offered so expertly.

"Oh, Jake," she called to him in a plea. He continued his stroking, causing electric impulses to shoot straight through her. He made her ache. He made her throb. The current traveled the length of her, spreading out with thrilling clarity until finally, finally, she reached the potent, powerful end.

Cassie was awash with tingles, every nerve alert, awakened by Jake and his expert caresses. And she wanted more. She wanted Jake. She wanted to take him inside her, to feel him move, to feel him shudder, to give to him what he so profoundly had given to her.

He lifted up then, boldly, with unabashed desire evident in his dark, penetrating gaze. His body, glistening and gleaming, so perfect in his aroused state, beckoned her. He rasped out her name. ''Cassie?''

She'd never known a need so powerful before. Her desire for Jake overwhelmed her with its stark intensity. With labored breaths, she whispered in the darkened room, ''Hurry, cowboy.''

A low, sexy chuckle rumbled from his chest. ''Yes, ma'am,'' he said. He rose above her, all humor vanishing from his face, replaced by a glint of raw need. He came to her with reverence, with slow heat and long strides. Cassie's body adjusted, the fit more than perfect. She moved with him, their bodies fully in tune and the contact igniting sparks, little tiny explosions of earth-shattering pleasure. Cassie whimpered as he moved inside her, taking her higher yet.

She witnessed the grinding pleasure on his face, the restraint and the control he exhibited as he moved, bringing her with him with each earth-shattering thrust. Higher and higher, he brought her up, faster now. And harder.

It was almost too much to bear. Cassie had reached her highest peak, ready now for the climax.

They came apart at the same time, calling out each other's names, complete and fulfilled. The moment seemed suspended in time, that last final surge of passion before falling in a heap onto the bed. There were no other sounds to be heard, no other place and time existed, but this exact moment amid mingled breaths, pounding hearts and moist, sated bodies.

Jake held her in his arms, rolling slightly away to relieve her of his weight. He kissed her once again, nuzzling her ear then laid back, fully spent. "Oh, man," he groaned on a slow breath, then reached out for her. "You okay, Cassie?"

"Mmm, great." There wasn't an adjective in the dictionary that could adequately describe the intensity of what Cassie was feeling right now, great being an incredible understatement. But their lovemaking had been so much more, too much for Cassie to start analyzing now. She'd done enough analyzing in her lifetime. Tonight she wanted to relish being in Jake's arms, relish what had just happened between them, without worry, condemnations or fear.

Jake lay behind her, holding her in a warm embrace. She heard him take a deep breath then let it out slowly. "I want to stay the night, honey."

It was a question, not a demand. And she knew the implication. Jake wanted to make love to her again. The thought warmed her heart and thrilled her, as well. She was powerless to deny him anything tonight. She'd have to face leaving him in the morning, but that was hours away. For tonight she'd grant herself this time alone with him.

Together they'd make a memory to last her a lifetime.

"Stay."

Streaming sunlight cast a glow in the room, a yellow hue of color and warmth that brought Cassie up from her bed. Hazy, she opened her eyes slowly, yawned and lifted her arms up over her head in a fully extended stretch. Peering to her side, she noted Jake was gone. She lifted his pillow and breathed in his scent, remnants of his spicy aftershave remained, reminding her of the night they'd shared making love.

Cassie closed her eyes as emotions ran deep. She knew her instincts had been right in not trusting herself with Jake. Last night had been a mistake, but ironically she had no regrets. How could she when every cell in her body rejoiced and every tiny ache she felt was an instant reminder of what they'd shared. With her permission, Jake had ravaged her, thrilling her at every turn, making all her fantasies come true. But Jake was gone now. It came as no surprise. They'd made no commitment to each other. Both knew their lives were separate, their dreams different and their futures had no chance of entwining. Yet neither had been strong enough to hold back, to do the sensible thing, to step away from each other. They'd shared one incredible, memorable night that she vowed to neither forget nor regret.

Cassie rose from the bed, stretched again, working out kinks, and wandered into the bathroom. She needed a long, hot shower before she made the trek back to Los Angeles. With the wedding over and Brian and Alicia on their honeymoon, Cassie could concentrate on her own plans. She had a new job waiting for her and all that went along with relocating to a new place. She'd put all her efforts in that and try to get past the amazing weekend she'd spent with Jake Griffin.

She looked into the mirror and gasped, startled, not by her image, but what was written across the mirror in bold red lipstick, her lipstick. "Come to the rodeo today."

Cassie's mouth dropped open. She wasn't expecting this, not at all. She'd slept in his arms throughout the night, being held in his tight embrace, but he hadn't once brought up the future, the very near future. He hadn't spoken about today, of saying a last goodbye.

She'd resigned herself to leaving Jake and this weekend

behind her. But those words, so simple yet so compelling, stirred her heart. To see Jake one more time. To see him do what he does best, well…maybe what he does second best, she thought wryly, would be too great a temptation to resist.

It would be a mistake to go. She thought of a dozen reasons why it wouldn't be wise to see her cowboy in action. It would be better just to end it here and now. The sensible thing to do would be to check out of the hotel, get into her car and drive five hours southwest to Los Angeles without looking back.

She stared once again at the lipstick staining the mirror as sensations ripped through her, quick flashes of this weekend and how Jake had been there for her every time she seemed to need him.

Like a white knight.

"'Come to the rodeo today,'" she murmured, a finger tracing the words slanting over the mirror.

And while her mind screamed a loud, impending no, her heart pounded out another message entirely. She'd go to the rodeo today and see Jake one more time.

Cassie planted herself down on a stadium bench at the River Stampede Rodeo. The pass Jake had left for her at the gate would give her the best view of the events, being closest to the chutes, in the V.I.P section, the ticket taker had stated with a wide smile. Cassie sat, her back to the hot afternoon sun, amid the dust of dry earth and the smell of ranch animals penned up in their stalls. The arena, only half a mile from the riverfront hotels, swarmed with people. She peered at the crowd of smiling faces, the majority of them jeans-clad and wearing Western hats, all anticipating the upcoming events. The stadium began filling up and Cassie moved over when an older man took a seat next to her.

"Appreciate it," he said with a tip of his white hat. She

smiled, noting the man had a rugged face, weathered with deep lines around his eyes; a man who had obviously enjoyed the outdoors most of his life. "First time to the rodeo?" he asked.

Surprised by his quick appraisal, she chuckled. "How did you know?"

"Got the look of a first-timer, is all."

"I've always wanted to come, just never had the chance before."

"Sit back and enjoy yourself," he said. "First timers are always in for a treat."

Cassie knew seeing Jake again would be a treat, but a forbidden one. She shouldn't have come. She could have been halfway back to Los Angeles by now, tying up loose ends and getting ready for her new job. Yet she was here and anxious to watch Jake compete.

An hour later Cassie gasped in horror as a bareback rider was tossed off a bucking bronco right in front of her section of seats. The cowboy flew high in the air before landing on the hard-packed dirt. He stayed there for a while before being helped up.

"Do you think he'll be all right?" she asked, turning to the man seated beside her.

"Sure enough. He'll be sore as hell, but he's not limping, so I imagine he'll be right as rain. He won't feel the true brunt of that fall for about twenty years or so." The man winked.

Cassie nodded, wondering if Jake's event would be as risky. She didn't think she could sit here and watch while he put himself in danger. From all she knew of the rodeo, which wasn't too much, she believed roping calves wasn't so much about danger but skill and timing.

Minutes later they announced the calf roping event and Cassie came to full attention. She watched patiently as the first three cowboys entered their times. But then they announced Jake's name and Cassie rose from her seat, her heart fluttering when she caught sight of him in the chute.

The impact at seeing Jake again was even more potent, more heart-wrenching, than she'd anticipated. She told herself to leave now, to get out while she still could, but Cassie didn't have that much willpower. Mesmerized, she watched him mounted up on his horse, sitting tall with rope in hand and one smaller one between his teeth, ready to compete.

It happened so fast, the calf dashed from the chute and Jake tossed the rope, jumped down from his horse and raced over to "flank the calf," a means of throwing the calf down, Cassie learned from her rodeo friend seated beside her. In a whirlwind of efficient motion, Jake tied up three of the calf's legs then bounded up with arms outstretched, signaling the judges that he'd completed the run. All in all, it took a matter of seconds, but Cassie's keen sense told her those seconds were profound, and not just for Jake.

The scoreboard flashed. Seven point five seconds, the best score posted yet. Jake tossed his hat in the air, waving to the crowd, obviously extremely pleased with his score. Cheers went up all around the arena.

Cassie kept her eyes focused on Jake, watching him take long, purposeful strides, retrieving his hat from the ground then jamming it back on his head. He gave the crowd one last wave before disappearing into the chutes again.

She swallowed hard, slammed her eyes shut, then felt herself swaying. This couldn't be happening. Not now, not with all the plans she'd made for her future.

"Whoa, little lady." A strong hand righted her.

She opened her eyes to find her rodeo friend beside her, marked concern etched in his crinkled eyes. "You all right?"

"Uh, no," she said softly. "I'm not all right. I have to go," she whispered. "I have to get out of here."

Cassie pushed her way out of the aisle, ran down the steps of the stadium and raced to her car in the dust-laden parking lot. She fumbled with the lock, then opened the door and sat down in the seat, her heart racing with dread. She wiped a stray tear from her cheek and started the engine.

The motor revved to life.

But Cassie only sat there, in stunned silence, her mind fighting a losing battle with her heart. She didn't want this. She couldn't believe her bad luck. She'd promised herself she wouldn't fall victim again. But all of her resolve had crumbled like unsteady walls in an earthquake. She'd never felt this way before, this quivering nerve-racking, all-out powerful jolt that hit her with incredible impact. She knew it meant only one thing.

She'd fallen deeply in love with Jake Griffin.

Five

Cassie pulled off Highway 395 onto a private paved road that led to another road, this one taking her deeper into the Carson Valley and closer to Anderson Ranch. Packed up to the ceiling with boxes of her belongings, she'd driven her Bug for over eight hours, leaving her family, friends and Los Angeles behind. She'd said a sorrowful goodbye to Brian and Alicia earlier this morning, each one misty-eyed, each one trying to be happy for her. She'd made a promise to Brian that she'd call often and that she'd be fine. Not to worry.

Her brother had only grimaced, giving her a tight squeeze.

Once she'd gotten out of the city, she'd felt better, brighter, and a little less sad. And now, seeing the open spaces, the tall meadows groomed only by animals grazing the land with a backdrop of mountains and clear skies devoid of smog, Cassie smiled.

She drove her Volkswagen Bug through wide white

arches that claimed Anderson Ranch with big, bold, black letters. Cassie drove farther then braked to a quick stop when she viewed the ranch house.

Visions of the television show "Dallas" came to mind, of the ranch named Southfork, and she nearly expected to see J.R. Ewing stepping out of the double doors. The house, more a mansion of sorts, stood in the center of what Cassie believed to be the largest ranch she'd ever seen. The acreage that surrounded the house seemed to go on and on until only the tall, pine-dotted mountains called it to a halt. And the house itself was stately with broad white columns, a two-story combination of adobe and masonry that spelled wealth and elegance.

This is where she'd work. This is where she'd put the past behind her. This is where she'd try to forget about Jake Griffin, the man who kept popping into her life to break her heart. It had been three weeks since she'd seen him—three of the longest weeks of her life. Cassie's focus now had to be on her new job and her new living arrangements. She hoped to fit in well and maybe even make a few new friends along the way.

She'd make a fresh start.

Cassie parked the car and approached the door, her stomach clenching. Nerves, she told herself. Before she could knock, the door opened. "Miss Munroe?"

A tall, tanned man with salt-and-pepper hair studied her. His face appeared rigid, as though he didn't know what a friendly smile could do, and his dark eyes seemed relentless. His eagle-like scrutiny was tempered only by the quiet tone of his voice.

Cassie's stomach did a little tumble. She'd been queasy all morning and she attributed the sensation to the stress of the move, the tearful farewell and the long drive. Looking at this man only heightened her queasiness. "Yes, I'm Cassandra Munroe."

He nodded and put out his hand. "John T. Anderson."

"Oh, uh, Mr. Anderson." Cassie took his hand and engaged in a firm shake. "It's nice to meet you."

He backed away from the door, allowing her entrance. "Come in."

She followed him into the parlor, but he didn't offer her a seat. He turned when he reached the mantel of a gigantic, white-stone fireplace. "You come highly recommended. I understand Lottie, my…well, she used to be my assistant until the fool woman decided to retire. Lottie Fairchild says you're from around here."

"Yes, sir." *Sir* seemed to fit. The man commanded respect. Cassie's stomach did another little flip-flop. "I was born and raised just outside of Reno. I lived there for twelve years. I've always wanted to come back."

"Good. I like that. Don't place much trust in city folk. We got a big spread here. We're a stock contract ranch. We raise bucking broncos mostly, to breed, to sell and to rent out to the rodeo. It's a place where rodeo animals come to rest up during the off-season or between rodeo runs. Got some steer and calves here, too. There're a lot of transactions going on all the time." He sighed, glancing at her as if suddenly suspicious. "You're almost a mite too pretty to be an accountant."

Cassie blushed, the heat rising up her neck to burn her cheeks and adding anxiety to her already-blinking stomach. She didn't know how to respond. Was he giving her a compliment or doubting her ability? "I have a head for numbers. Always have. For instance, I can tell you that I drove exactly four hundred, thirty-six miles to get here. I passed five waterholes on my way in, counted twelve oaks lining the entrance to the property, you've got seven buildings including

the house on your land and that Garth Brooks is probably
your favorite country singer.''

He raised a brow in question.

''You've got four of his CDs behind you on the mantel.''

''Oh, Lottie gave them to me.'' Then the man cracked a
small smile, enough for Cassie to see his dark eyes light up
some and his face soften. ''That's not bad. You're gonna fit
in around here, Miss Munroe.''

Cassie grinned. She'd passed the test, she supposed, but
her stomach wasn't smiling. And now her head felt funny,
as if she were floating on air. She put a hand to her belly,
wishing this wasn't happening. ''Uh-oh. I don't feel so
good.''

Mr. Anderson reached for her, taking her arm. ''Darn my
bad manners. I didn't offer you a seat or something to drink.
You've been on the road for hours. What can I do?''

''The bathroom?''

He held her arm and guided her to a room just off the
parlor. ''Let me know if you need anything.''

Cassie barely made it inside to lock the door before she
heaved. Her muscles clenched and when she was all done,
her stomach was better and she felt human again. Except
for the embarrassment. Well, she sure made a memorable
first impression, didn't she?

Cassie washed her face then reached into her bag to reap-
ply lip gloss. She ran a brush through her hair, tidied up her
skirt and blouse, then walked back into the parlor.

''In here,'' she heard Mr. Anderson call.

She headed for the sound of his voice, finding him in a
large room on the opposite side of the house. Mr. Anderson
sat in a bulky, chocolate-brown leather chair behind a no-
nonsense mahogany desk. Dark panels made up three of the
walls with inlaid shelves housing a mass of books. Deep

burgundy-velour drapes partially covered two bay windows that looked out upon the ranch.

Cassie would say it was definitely a man's room.

"Come in and have a seat. Feeling better?"

"Yes, much better. I think it was car sickness or something." She took a seat in a smaller leather chair facing him.

"Good. Marie is setting up a light supper on the veranda. And after we eat, I'll show you to the guest house. We just need to go over some things in your contract and have you sign on the dotted line. Lottie assures me you're agreeable to the conditions?"

"Yes, it's all been worked out."

He nodded. "Take a look at this." He turned the contract on his desk her way and gave it a little shove. "Read it over and let me know if you have any questions."

Cassie took a moment to read what was expected of her. The salary was more than generous, considering she'd be living rent-free in the guest house, and everything else seemed to be in order. "No, no questions. This is what we agreed upon." Anxious to start her new job, Cassie picked up a pen and signed the document.

"Great," Mr. Anderson said, standing. "You must be hungry. Let's go get us some grub."

Cassie stood in the center of the "guest house" living room, shaking her head. The place wasn't exactly what she'd expected. She'd had visions of a small, cozy, cabin-like home where there would be no mistaking typical ranch-style living. But this house was decorated in modern rustic, with adobe-colored walls and the furniture barely hinting at its Western heritage. There was an open, airy feel to the place that sent endorphins swimming through her body. The minute she'd walked in, she knew she'd love living here. And the place was actually larger than most L.A condos.

Highlighting the living room was a red-stone fireplace and two matching sofas set in soft hues of beige and peach. The house had two good-size bedrooms, a master with its own bath, a full kitchen with a nook overlooking the mountains to the east and a full dining area. There was a small built-in bar halfway between the living and dining areas. The other bedroom Mr. Anderson had designated as her office complete with a computer, fax machine and two phone lines.

He'd explained that Lottie had done her work in an office in the main house, but both had figured Cassie would like her privacy. He'd also explained there were no set hours to the job. When she was through with her work, she was free for the rest of the day. He didn't expect her to work on the weekends, unless there was something pressing that couldn't wait until Monday.

Cassie let out a long, contented sigh, feeling more at peace now that the initial meeting was over. Her stomach was much better and the anxiety over her job was all but gone.

Her car was parked inside a small garage attached to the house. She'd brought in only one suitcase, far too tired to think about unpacking tonight. She'd worry about the rest of her stuff tomorrow. Cassie planned to take a quick shower, change into her nightclothes and go straight to bed. Glancing out the window, she chuckled softly. ''The sun's barely setting and you're going to bed.''

This was what she'd wanted—to live easier, simpler and with less stress. Yet, she couldn't help feeling a bit lonely. ''Tomorrow, Cassie Munroe, you are going to start your life.''

Jake Griffin turned the key in the lock and entered the dark solitude of his home. Exhausted from the long, grueling drive back from Colorado, all he wanted to do was to strip out of his clothes and get some sleep. He littered clothes from the front room, tossing his boots and shirt aside, his pants made it to the hallway and, by the time he got to his bed, he was down to his briefs. He tossed the covers aside and climbed in, resting his head upon his pillow and closing his eyes.

A familiar scent drifted by, a soft, subtle, fragrant smell that brought back memories of the woman he'd been trying darn hard to forget.

Cassie Munroe.

Jake squeezed his eyes shut tighter and scoffed at his addled brain. Fatigue, he figured, lowered your resistance, because he'd made a great effort in the past three weeks to put the woman and that weekend behind him.

A soft feminine sigh, the barest of sound, had him turning toward the far end of his king-size bed. Jake blinked and rolled a bit closer, wondering if the apparition was real or some trick of his imagination. No trick, he realized immediately. There *was* a woman in his bed.

And as he took a better look, relying on a slim sliver of moonlight edging its way into the window, there was no mistaking who she was.

Cassie Munroe.

A dozen emotions whirled around, creating havoc in his head, his gut and his groin. Stunned, Jake could only stare. Cassie was in a deep sleep. He'd watched her sleep before and the sight of her sexy body, so serene and peaceful in his bed, brought forth many questions. Why was she here? Why had she come to him?

He'd been royally ticked off when she hadn't come to the rodeo as he'd asked. He didn't quite know what he'd say to her, what he'd expected, but he had wanted to see her again. Anger had surfaced then and all of his stubborn pride wouldn't allow him to call her in Los Angeles. He figured he'd served his purpose by taking her to her brother's wedding. She'd had no use for him after that.

Jake was accustomed to being abandoned. He'd dealt with rejection all of his life. He wasn't that needy kid, looking for love any longer. In truth, he scoffed at the notion. In Jake Griffin's world, love didn't exist.

But after the incredible night they'd shared making love, Jake hadn't expected Cassie to run out on him. Okay, maybe his ego had been bruised. But he'd wanted to say something to her that day. He'd wanted to ask her if he could see her again if he happened to visit California?

Hell, he didn't know. The woman made him nuts.

And now, she was lying next to him in his bed.

Jake edged himself closer and the immediate impact, the way he responded to her, had him silently swearing. His body hadn't forgotten her. Hard and tight, Jake rolled away, a mental debate going on in his head whether he should wake her or not. He ruled in favor of sleep. Morning was just hours away.

He'd find out soon enough what Cassie Munroe wanted from him.

Six

Cassie had slept the sleep of the dead. She'd never been so tired in her life. She lay there reluctant to open her eyes to welcome the new day. Just another five minutes, she told herself, then she'd bounce out of bed and start unpacking. The thought made her sigh and she rolled onto her side, grasping her pillow, snuggling in, but something solid, unyielding and vaguely familiar stopped her.

A soft kiss brushed her lips. "Morning, Cassie."

Startled, Cassie blinked her eyes open. Hazy from sleep, she fought to focus, to make sense of it all as quick, dreadful sensations ripped straight through her. She knew those lips, that deep voice, the appealing scent of the man she'd been dreaming about. This was no dream. He was real, and holding her in his arms.

What piece of this puzzle had she forgotten?

She pulled back and away quickly, grasping her pillow

tight. "Jake? W-what are you doing here? And w-why are you in my b-bed?"

"*Your bed?*" Jake chuckled, coming closer, running a finger down her face and tucking strands of her hair behind her ear, sending shivers along her spine. "Sweetheart, did you mix your allergy pills with liquor again last night?"

"No. No, I most certainly did not. This is my bed, Jake. And what on earth are you doing here?" She peered out the bedroom doorway, but couldn't see the front door. She knew she'd locked everything up tight last night before turning in. She glanced at her bedroom window, as well—still closed. It was way too early in the morning for Cassie to try to figure out this mystery. She narrowed her eyes. "How did you get in?"

"The usual way, with a key."

Cassie sat up straighter in the bed, dragging the covers to her chin. Her heart pumped overtime, seeing him again, recalling the exquisite feel of his lips on hers just seconds ago, but she couldn't dwell on those sensations now. She had more pressing things to think about, such as how he'd found her. "But how, I mean—"

"I live here," he said simply, as though he expected her to know that. "This is my home."

Baffled, Cassie opened her mouth but no words sputtered out. He lives here? How could that be?

"You're in my bed, Cassie." He shot her a sexy grin, as if to say he didn't know her game but he'd be willing to play, anyway.

"But, but…Mr. Anderson said—"

"What does my father have to do with this?" Jake's expression suddenly changed. No longer amused, he peered at her with dark intensity. "Tell me, Cassie. What did my father do this time?"

"Your *father?*"

"Yes, dammit. John T. Anderson is my father."

"Oh." She tried absorbing that fact. Mr. Anderson was Jake's father. Cassie found it hard to believe any of this. Waking up in a strange bed only to find Jake Griffin lying next to her was one thing, but to learn that this was his home, and that her employer was Jake's father, well, that little bit of information completely blew her mind. She felt as though she'd been time warped into another dimension. "He, uh, he hired me. I work for him now."

Jake bounded out of bed, letting go a string of curses that would shock the toughest of longshoremen. She resisted covering her ears, but couldn't resist the view of Jake pacing the floor, nearly naked, wearing only his briefs.

Heavens, the man had a body on him. She hadn't forgotten how glorious he'd been to touch, the feel of his hot skin or the sultry passion they'd once shared.

Finally, Jake stopped pacing. With contained anger, he stared down at her. "So, you didn't come here to see me?"

Cassie shook her head slowly.

"And you didn't know I was John T. Anderson's son?"

She gave him another shake of the head.

"Wait a minute!" Jake peered at the bedroom, as if seeing it for the first time. His eyes darted from the nightstand to the dresser to the closet. He headed there first, sliding open the mirrored door. Empty. He opened dresser drawers, stuck his head into the bathroom and came out with fury in his eyes. "Sonofabitch! He's moved me out. He'd do anything to get me to live in the main house! *Anything*."

Cassie jumped out of bed, tangling with the sheet and finally giving up. She was decently covered in her pajama tank and shorts. Jake had seen her in less, much less. "Jake, are you saying your father offered me your house to live in?"

With hands firmly on hips, he nodded. "That's exactly what I'm saying."

"Oh, uh, I truly had no idea. I'm sorry. I'll leave. I haven't even unpacked yet. I'll find another place to stay."

Jake put up his hands. "Don't leave, Cassie, and don't be sorry. This is all John T.'s doing. Hell, it's not like I'm attached to this place or anything. But he's gonna get a piece of my mind regardless. This really has nothing to do with you. It's between John T. and me."

Jake began dressing, picking up his clothes that were scattered on the floor. With pants on and his shirt hanging from his shoulders Cassie watched him yank the front door open and storm out. Between Jake Griffin and John T. Anderson, she didn't know which man was the most stubborn. Living here with both of them, she figured she'd soon find out.

That's if she decided to stay.

Cassie now had major doubts. She'd come here to start a new life, to put the mistakes in her past behind her. How could she do that with Jake Griffin, the source of her recent heartache, living here on the ranch? Yet, Cassie didn't have any place else to go. She'd given up her job and her apartment back in Los Angeles. She'd signed a contract with Mr. Anderson. As much as she hated to admit it, Cassie's options were limited. And once she'd given her word, she'd never backed out of a deal.

Small wonder her stomach began its blinking act once more. Seeing Jake again had wiped that contented feeling right out from under her. She still had trouble believing he lived here, on the ranch where she was to be employed. What were the odds of that? Mentally she calculated, her mind clicking away, but she didn't have the data to produce such odds though she knew it had to be pretty far out there.

She grabbed a pair of jeans, a shirt and fresh underwear from her luggage and headed to the shower. "No time for a queasy stomach, Cassie Munroe. You have too much to do today.''

Now, if her stomach, her head and her heart would only listen.

''Don't raise your voice to me, boy. Calm down and have a seat.''

Jake continued to pace in front of the desk in the study as John T. sat comfortably in his chair. The man had an uncanny way of manipulating situations. Jake figured it was the key to his success in business. John T. knew the odds and how to play them. ''I don't want to sit, dammit. I want answers. Why in hell did you move Cassie into my house?''

His father's brows lifted. ''Cassie?''

''Yeah, Cassie—the redhead sleeping in my bed.''

''Hmm.'' John T. rubbed his jaw. ''Exactly what time did you come home last night?''

''Two a.m.''

''Two, huh? Where did you sleep?''

Jake waved him off. He wasn't about to tell his father he'd slept next to Cassie all night long. He hadn't gotten but a few winks, too keyed up about her presence in his bed and the staggering, erotic possibilities. It was only by an ironclad will that Jake hadn't woken her in the night to continue what they'd started that night in her hotel room. ''None of your business.''

''It's my business if you go scaring off the new hired help.''

''I might have startled her this morning, but Cassie doesn't scare off easily. She's fine.''

His father blinked and Jake realized he might have said too much. ''Are you saying you know this girl?''

''Like I said, it's none of your business. So why'd you do it?''

"Hell, boy. How'd it look to have a pretty young woman living in this house alone with me? I had no choice but to give her the guest house. Lottie said it was the proper thing to do. Hell, if that woman hadn't up and retired on me, none of this would have been necessary, anyway."

"Yeah, well, if you weren't so dang stubborn, maybe Lottie wouldn't have taken an early retirement."

Anger flashed in John T.'s eyes, mixed with keen curiosity. "What's that supposed to mean?"

"Nothing. Forget I said anything." Jake wasn't here to reprimand his father on his relationship with Lottie. Though, if he ever had another opportunity, he'd be happy to tell the old man what a doggone fool he'd been in that regard.

John T. let out a long, exasperated sigh. "You weren't supposed to be home at all this weekend. I was planning on calling you today to give you the details. Hell, boy, if you'd only taken an interest in the ranch business, you'd have known I'd hired on some new help. And seeing as we've got twelve rooms in this house, I figured you could just as well bunk here. It's not as if you're home much, anyway."

That much was true. Jake hadn't ever felt as though Anderson Ranch was his home. He'd never felt he belonged here. Since John T. had brought him to Nevada, Jake had finished out his high school days here then spent the next five years away at college. When he returned, he'd taken up residence in the guest house, but he'd spent most of his time on the road with the rodeo.

"I guess I have no choice now. We both know it's a thirty-minute drive from town. There ain't a whole lot of rentals and none as nice as the guest house. I'm not about to send Cassie off packing somewhere. She came here with good intentions. Besides, knowing you, you probably included the living arrangements as part of the deal."

His father scratched his head. "You do know her, don't you?"

Jake relented. What difference did it make, anyway? He'd learned from his father's past secrets that you couldn't hide much in this world. Sooner or later the truth would come out. "Yes, I knew her in California."

"That was a long time ago." His father questioned him further with a long lingering look.

"And I met up with her at the rodeo last month in Laughlin. She was going to her brother's wedding and it was sort of a coincidence that we met."

"Sounds more like fate to me," John T. stated, his mind working overtime. Jake knew that particular expression and he didn't much like it. When his father twisted his mouth upward, eyes twinkling, Jake knew he probably shouldn't have given up so much information. "Well, I'll be damned."

Jake decided to ignore that look and the tone of his father's voice. "What room did you have my things moved into?"

"Your old room."

Jake nodded.

"It's not the end of the world, Jake. This is your house, too."

Jake walked out of the study, gritting his teeth. He didn't have any choice. Cassie would have the guest house. She'd be more comfortable there and she'd have a bit of privacy.

But hell, he didn't want to move into the main house. He'd avoided doing so for years. Now because of Cassie Munroe, the woman who'd entered his life twice before, he'd have to leave the guest house. Somehow she'd managed to turn his life upside down for a third time. He didn't want Cassie here. She was a distraction, a complication that he didn't need.

She was a woman hard to ignore, but once all this was straightened out, Jake was determined to steer clear of Cassie Munroe.

Cassie met up with Jake as soon as she climbed down the steps of the guest house. "I was coming over to see what I should do."

Jake stated calmly, "Start unpacking. You're staying here."

"But how can I when this is your home? I don't want to uproot you."

Jake's expression changed then, a twinkle gleaming in his dark, captivating eyes. He shot her a slow smile. "We could bunk together, Cassie," he said softly. "If that would make you feel better."

Heat climbed up her neck, not from embarrassment but from the memory of the "bunking" she'd done with Jake. She didn't want to give him any encouragement. Heavens, this was where she was going to work. She wanted to make a good impression and to do an excellent job. The last thing she needed right now was to complicate her life again with Jake. She'd examined the issue in her mind, weighing her options and coming up with only one viable choice: to stay. But she could and would distance herself from Jake. "Not a chance, cowboy."

His lighthearted demeanor didn't change. "Okay, then let's get you unpacked. Where's your gear?"

Cassie opened the garage door with the remote and her car appeared, crammed to its limit with her "stuff."

"I bet you've got a dozen clowns in there, too."

"They're hiding under the seat. I put all my furniture in storage. This was what's left."

Twenty minutes later, after Jake unloaded all the boxes in her car, Cassie handed him a tall glass of water as they stood in the kitchen. "Thanks for the help. I think I can manage from here."

Jake opened the refrigerator and shook his head. "Looks like you need some provisions."

"I was planning on driving into town this afternoon to pick up some groceries."

"I'm heading that way later. I can give you a lift."

It was a tempting offer, but Cassie couldn't accept. She was on her own now. She had to fend for herself and, quite honestly, she didn't want to get accustomed to having Jake around. Her heart still ached every time he showed up. Better to keep her mind focused on anything and everything but him. "No thanks. I'll be okay."

But suddenly Cassie wasn't okay. A wave of fatigue hit her and her legs nearly buckled. Light-headed, she closed her eyes and found herself swaying.

"Whoa, there." Jake grabbed her before she fell. He pressed her head into his chest and murmured quietly, "What's wrong?"

Still floating, she relished the solid feel of his chest and the support of his strong arms. "Dizzy."

He held her there, stroking her back gently. She heard the erratic rhythms of his heartbeat; the rapid pounding that flashed her eyes open. She looked up into his eyes and her head cleared instantly.

"Better?" he asked, concerned.

"Yeah, better."

"What happened?"

"I don't know. I felt faint for a second. I guess I'm just tired. I'll feel better once I eat something."

Jake didn't release his hold on her, instead his arms tightened around her waist. Cassie's heart raced like mad. Being in his arms brought back vivid memories of another time, when she'd been mesmerized by his charm, completely taken by his sweet regard. And judging by the hungry look he cast her, Cassie knew he was thinking the same thing. His gaze probed hers and he lowered his head, his lips just inches away. A different kind of dizziness swamped her, one that made her lose all good sense. She lifted up to meet him, but a racket at the front door made her jump back.

"Hello, there! Cassandra, are you in there? It's Lottie Fairchild." Soft knocking became a bit louder. "I brought breakfast, darlin'."

Cassie wiped her brow, feeling steady on her feet now. She didn't know what had just happened. One minute she was fine, the next she was so light-headed that she could barely stand up. Thank goodness Jake was there to catch her. And thank goodness Lottie Fairchild showed up in time to stop Cassie from making a mistake. She looked at Jake and shrugged. "Yes, I'll be right there, Mrs. Fairchild."

Cassie opened the door to a sweet-faced woman she presumed to be in her early sixties. She had light blond hair done up with a little flip at the shoulders, and beautiful amber eyes. Typical Western wear, a plaid shirt, new denim jeans and black boots, made up Lottie Fairchild's attire. "Hey, darlin'. I see you made it here all right yesterday." She held a basket filled with sweet muffins, corn cakes and jellies. "I hope you're hungry. I baked these fresh this morning."

"Oh, thank you. These look wonderful. It's nice to meet you, Mrs. Fairchild. Come in."

"It's Lottie to everyone but the tax collector." She winked, then noticed Jake standing at the back of the room. "Hey, Jake. I see you two have already been acquainted."

"Yes, uh, Jake helped bring in my boxes from the car."

"Morning, Lottie," Jake said, coming up to swipe two

muffins from the basket. "I sure have missed these muffins."

"You come on over to my place anytime and I'll bake them up fresh for you."

Jake nodded and strode to the door. "Thanks, Lottie. Gotta run. See you all later."

Lottie watched Jake leave. "That boy's forever running off someplace." She sighed and took a good look at Cassie. "You feeling all right?"

"Yes, just a bit tired. I didn't sleep well last night." Liar, she'd slept like a baby. That was why Cassie was so confused. She didn't understand her bout of fatigue this morning.

"Well, sure. That makes sense. Starting a new job, moving into a new place and all. We'll just have us something to eat, then if you're up to it, I'll show you the books."

"Oh, I'm up to it. I'm eager to get started."

Lottie Fairchild's daily training proved to be a blessing to Cassie. Lottie had come over each morning for the past three days, teaching Cassie about the transactions that went on with a stock contract ranch. She'd sit with her at the computer, but her training went much further than numbers on a screen. She'd relate stories about the animals, how they were acquired, which bucking horses were worth the most, which mare had the sweetest of temperaments, and how she'd been there to witness the birthing of the latest colt or filly.

"You ought to see Pistol Pete. He's a dandy," Lottie said once they were through with their paperwork.

"Who's Pistol Pete?" Cassie asked.

"He's just the sweetest piebald colt you'd ever want to see. Born a month and a half ago. I'm surprised Jake or John T. hasn't taken you on a tour of the ranch yet."

"I haven't seen Jake all week," Cassie said, trying for nonchalance. This was what she wanted, after all. She didn't need Jake interfering in her life. She'd vowed to keep it civil between them whenever they were together, but it would end there. Jake was nowhere to be found these days.

"He'll be back today most likely. He's riding rodeo again. That boy's determined to win the championship. I think he might do it this year."

"That's what he wants, right?"

"Right, though he's probably doing it for all the wrong reasons. But that's between him and John T."

"Somebody say my name?" John T.'s voice filtered through the house.

Cassie bounded up from her seat at the computer and went to the front door. "Hello, Mr. Anderson." She let him in.

He yanked off his hat, holding it at his side. "We're not formal around here. It's John T. And my son says you go by Cassie?"

"Jake said that?" Cassie wondered what else Jake had told his father about their relationship. Heavens, she didn't want to think about that right now.

John T. eyed her for a moment, gauging her reaction. "May I call you Cassie?"

"Of course. I'd like that."

"I came to invite you to supper tonight. Figured I've given you enough time to settle in. Everything suit your needs?"

"Yes, I love it here. The place is great. And Lottie's been by every day to train me. I think I'm catching on."

Lottie entered the living room. "You're more than catching on. Another day or two and you won't need my help at all."

"Morning, Lottie," John T. said, his eyes just a bit

brighter as they rested on the blond-headed woman. "I just came by to invite Cassie to supper tonight. You come, too, Lottie."

Lottie smiled. "Sorry, John T. I have plans tonight."

John T. grimaced and an awkward silence ensued as the two stared at each other. "Fine. I'll see you tonight at seven, Cassie."

"Thank you. I'll be there."

When John T. walked out the door, Cassie couldn't help but grin at Lottie. "What was that all about?"

Lottie waved a hand in the air. "That man thinks a woman's got to jump when he says jump. About time someone taught him a lesson or two." She mimicked him. "'You come, too, Lottie.' Tell me, is that a way for a man to invite a lady to supper?"

"You're in love with him!" Cassie blurted. She couldn't help notice the sparks flying between the two of them and she felt comfortable enough with Lottie to speak her mind.

"Sweet darlin', a woman's got to be a damn fool to love that man. I've worked for him for twenty-two years. I know him better than he knows himself and believe me, he's no bargain."

Before Cassie could reply, her stomach clenched. Each day she had hoped to be the last with her nervous stomach, but each day she'd been disappointed. Today was no exception. The cramping tightened and she groaned, "Oh, no, not again." She headed straight for the bathroom.

Lottie called, sincere concern in her voice, "I sure hope it ain't my muffins making you sick every morning, darlin'."

Later that afternoon Cassie strode out her door, needing a breath of air. She'd been diligent at the computer for days, learning the new program she'd be using for the ranch business. Lottie had been a great help, but she'd also been right about Cassie needing to know more about the ranch itself. She needed to see it firsthand. So once her bout of queasiness had subsided, Cassie had changed into worn-out jeans and an old tank top. She laced up her new black boots, frowning at the thought of getting them dusty, but as they say, when in Rome… She walked across the road then headed down a path toward the outer buildings she assumed were barns and stables.

"Need a lift?"

Cassie peered up to find Jake mounted on a big black horse with beautiful white markings on its snout. Her heart pounded in her chest seeing Jake look so at ease upon that massive animal. It suited him, as though horse and man were one, both moving fluidly with grace and agility.

Cassie kept walking, Jake and his horse following at her side. "I thought I'd take a look around. Haven't seen much of the ranch since I got here."

Jake squinted into the sunlight then lowered the brim of his hat. "Lottie gave me a sharp tongue-lashing for not showing you around. You can't see the ranch on foot, honey. There's more than thirty thousand acres here." He reached down and put out his hand. "Climb on up."

Cassie cringed, staring up at Jake. "What's wrong with your truck?"

He laughed. "Nothing, truck's running just fine. But if you want to really see the ranch and the animals, you have to see it my way."

Cassie continued to stare at the towering horse. "I've never ridden before."

Jake's brow lifted. "A small-town girl like you hasn't been astride a horse?"

"That's right. I'm a small-town girl at heart, but I've never lived on a ranch before, Jake."

He gestured with a quick swipe of his hand. ''Come on up. Shadow and I will make it painless.''

Cassie pursed her lips. She didn't like the look of the stallion, yet she knew Jake to be an expert horseman. She'd be safe with him in that regard, but riding double with Jake might create another kind of danger. ''O-okay. But you're going to have to help me up.''

Jake dismounted and moved to her side. ''Put your left foot in the stirrup and swing your right leg over the saddle.''

Cassie turned and looked up into his eyes. ''Where will you be?''

''Right behind you.'' With both hands, he grasped her waist. ''Ready?''

She followed his instructions and before she knew it she was cradled in Jake's arms, his thighs pressing against hers, her bottom tucked up against his groin. Her body prickled with sensation as he reached around to grab the reins, brushing the undersides of her breasts. Cassie moaned silently.

Not a good thing.

''Just relax,'' he said softly in her ear. ''The nickel tour starts right now.''

Cassie was a fool to let him talk her into this. She wasn't over him, not by a long shot. Seeing him again, living on the same ranch, *his* ranch, and spending time with him like this, could only lead to more heartache. Cassie knew enough about Jake Griffin to know he wasn't an easy man. He had issues, with his father for one and with trust for another. He was just as much the loner he'd been when she'd met him in high school. He'd been sorely disillusioned by events Cassie had yet to learn, but they were there, always, in his eyes, the firm set of jaw and in the way he had of putting up defenses.

She'd vowed to steer clear of troubled men and Jake Griffin was first on that list. Cassie knew he'd never let her in, never put her above his list of priorities. Yet, being held in his arms, having his body so close, had a way of making her forget everything in her head. "Jake, maybe this isn't a good idea."

"I've got you, Cassie. There's nothing to be afraid of."

He's got her.

That was everything to be afraid of.

Seven

"**N**ormally, I eat in the kitchen, but Marie thought since you're the invited guest, we should do it up nice in here," John T. stated.

Cassie glanced around at the austere dining room. The room was dark with stately elegance that Cassie thought didn't quite fit the rest of the house. Deep-red velvet curtains, walnut oak crown molding and the most intimidating furniture Cassie had ever seen made up the bulk of the large room. She was seated to the right of John T. and there were seven empty chairs around the table, with the exception of one other place setting. Cassie assumed that had to be for Jake.

"You want the truth, John T?" Cassie had to force his first name out. In her mind, he was still Mr. Anderson, her staunch employer.

There was interest in his dark eyes. "Always."

"This is...nice. But this room is nearly bigger than my

old apartment in Los Angeles. I'd rather have our meal in the kitchen, too.''

John T. cracked an iota of a smile. He stood and grabbed both their plates. ''Well, let's go.''

Five minutes later, and much to Marie's dismay, she and John T. had plates of food in front of them in the bright, cheerful kitchen. They began their meal with a glass of red wine.

''Make a toast, Cassie,'' he ordered, and she was starting to believe John T.'s bark was much worse than his bite.

She lifted her glass. ''To new beginnings,'' she said, and they put their glasses together before taking a sip.

''Ah, if only I could go back,'' he said softly.

''Back?''

John T. nodded. ''We don't get the luxury of second chances, do we?''

''Boy, I sure wouldn't mind a second chance or two,'' she admitted.

He waved her off. ''You? You're a young, intelligent woman, Cassie. You haven't begun to live yet. But me, I've made a lifetime of mistakes. And I'm afraid I'm paying the price.'' With a shrug, his rigid demeanor melted away and Cassie saw regret enter his eyes. ''Maybe it's what I deserve.''

Cassie sipped her wine. ''You're a success, John T. You have a wonderful house and the ranch is…well, Jake took me on a tour today. I'm impressed with all you've done here.''

''Jake, huh? Tell me. Is he treating you all right?''

More than all right, Cassie wouldn't announce. They'd been together for two hours this afternoon, riding his stallion, viewing the land. Every time they'd dismounted to stretch their legs or to catch a better view of the grazing animals, they fought their attraction to each other. Like a magnet, Cassie felt drawn to Jake and her instincts told her he'd felt the strong pull, too. They'd almost kissed, Jake coming up from behind as they stood in a tall meadow amid a blue sky, the surroundings quietly serenaded by rustling leaves and the flap of their clothes against the breeze. Cassie had come to her senses and stepped away, out of his reach, hoping to break the mood, to keep Jake from taking more of her heart.

"Jake is treating me just fine."

"That's good. As you might have guessed, he and I don't see eye-to-eye on much of anything."

Cassie remained quiet. She'd been curious about their relationship, or rather what seemed more like their estrangement, but she'd never pry. She'd let John T. do all the talking and listen to as much as he was willing to share.

"It goes way back. I've made my share of mistakes with that boy, I'll admit. I'll even say, I didn't treat him fairly, but I was in a hard place. I'd been a rodeo rider myself. Not a calf roper, like Jake, but I wrestled steers. Never did make it to the championship, but, I had the ladies lining up, anyway. I met Jake's mother at the rodeo one day. Man, oh, man, she was a beauty and I was a young randy cowboy, pretty full of myself. Only problem was, I was also a married man by then. You're gonna find this out sooner or later, anyway, so it might as well come from me. Nine months later, give or take a few weeks, both Jake's mother and my wife had babies. Both were boys and both were mine." Eyes the color of dark coal gauged her reaction, perhaps looking for signs of shock or maybe even disdain.

Cassie gulped down the wine in her mouth. She couldn't judge John T., but yes, he had shocked her. And yes, the pieces of Jake's torn-up life were beginning to take shape in her mind. "I knew Jake when he lived in a foster home. We were just kids."

"He told me he'd known you back then, but that's all I know."

Cassie didn't offer more. There would be time for explanations someday...maybe. This conversation wasn't about her, but about John T.'s relationship with his son.

He explained, "I had a wife and a new baby of my own. I offered to pay for Jake's care and to send money to Isabella, but she wouldn't hear of it. She didn't want my money. I couldn't give her what she wanted."

Cassie lifted a finger in his direction. "You."

He nodded. "There's more, but the bottom line is, Jake has never forgiven me."

"I'm sorry," she said with all sincerity. "But what happened to your wife and son?"

All the life drained from John T.'s face. "John Junior died in a boating accident when he was sixteen. His mother never got over it. She blamed me for everything and left three months later."

Cassie's heart ached for the tragic loss, for the boy and the pain John T. must have suffered losing both his son and his wife. In the span of a few short months John T.'s life had changed drastically. She couldn't find the words to express her sorrow, but John T.'s sharp eyes softened on her as if he could read her thoughts.

"I'm just telling you this so you understand. From time to time, Jake and I butt heads. It's not a pretty sight but I don't want you to worry about it. Lottie was good at putting us both in our place. Without her, Lord only knows what'll happen around here."

"Hmm. From what I know of her, she's a special woman."

John T. grunted and the conversation died the minute Jake stepped into the room with a tall, leggy blonde on his arm.

"Look who I picked up just outside of town." Jake's smile was wide, warm and welcoming.

Cassie's heart hammered with dread and immediate pain slashed straight through her at seeing the young woman, obviously enamored with Jake, draped across his arm. And Cassie had never seen Jake with such an open, unguarded expression on his face before. He appeared completely taken by the young woman.

Was this the same man who just hours ago had tried to make a move on her?

John T. stood up immediately and grinned wide, also, completely and pleasantly delighted. What was with the Anderson men tonight and who was this woman?

"Hi, Uncle John." She reached up to kiss John T.'s cheek.

"Hey, Suzette, darlin'." He squeezed her tight with a big bear hug. "What're you doing in town? Shouldn't you be in school?"

"I'm on spring break." She glanced at Jake with total adoration in her eyes. "I tagged after Jake, so I could come say hello."

Jake caught Cassie's stare, the evidence of her reaction probably written all over her face. He winked and shot her a knowing smile. Darn it all, Cassie was terrible at hiding her emotions.

"Where are my manners? Suzette, this is Cassandra Munroe. She's taking over your mother's job. Cassie, meet Suzette Fairchild, Lottie's youngest and my godchild."

Cassie blinked her surprise and stood to greet Lottie's daughter, making sure to avoid Jake's gaze. "Nice to meet you. I've only just met your mother and I already adore her."

Suzette flashed a big smile. "Mama has that effect on people."

Suzette probably did, too. Not only was she stunning with long blond hair, healthy tanned skin and bright blue eyes, but she had a sweet-natured personality.

Jake kept grinning at her.

Cassie found it quite annoying.

"Just wanted to say hey to y'all. I can't stay. Mama would have my hide. I'm already late and we're going out for supper."

"You come back now and see us again real soon, all right?" John T. said. "I want to hear all about those college boys you're dating. I bet you're breaking hearts, darlin'."

The sound of her beautiful laughter echoed against the kitchen walls. She answered John T. but her focus was entirely on Jake. "Oh, Uncle John, I don't have any boyfriends right now."

Suzette said her farewells and Jake walked her out to her car. Cassie sat down, before she fell down. She didn't like the emotions rolling around in her gut any more than she liked seeing Jake so taken with Lottie's youngest daughter.

"That girl's a ray of sunshine," John T. said after taking his seat again.

Cassie couldn't argue with that. She was genuine, the real article, and probably attracted men to her without batting an eyelash. "She seems close to Jake."

"Jake thinks of her as a little sister, Cassie. She sort of latched on to him when he came to live here."

"Still latching, I see." She'd never been one to hold her tongue, either. Darn, she was going to have to work on that.

John T. held back a smile. "It's nothing to worry about, Cassie."

"Who said I was worried?"

Heck, she didn't want to complicate her life with Jake Griffin any more than he wanted to strike up a relationship with her. She shouldn't have let her emotions rip into her that way. She had no claim on Jake. He could see anyone he pleased.

John T. glanced at his plate. "Food's getting cold. We'd better eat up."

"Sure." She peered down at sliced brisket, creamed corn and mashed potatoes, wondering how she was going to make a dent in the enormous meal. She'd just lost her appetite. "This looks great."

The next morning Cassie had assumed her position in the office, seated next to Lottie, facing the computer and a mass of paperwork on the desk that no longer appeared threatening. Thanks to Lottie, Cassie had a much better understanding of what it took to run a contract stock ranch with twenty-plus employees.

"This is your last day of training, Cassie. You've caught on so fast I'm truly impressed by you. Come to think of it, I'm pretty darn impressed with myself for hiring you." Lottie chuckled. "Of course, if you ever need anything, you just have to give me a call."

"I'm going to miss seeing you every day. Of course, now you'll have more time to spend with your daughter. I met her last night. She's very sweet."

Lottie had done wonders in cheering Cassie up each morning, bringing in home-baked goods along with her home-baked friendly attitude. She'd been welcome company even on the days when Cassie's stomach was on the blink, or when she'd felt so honest-to-gosh tired she didn't know how she'd make it through the morning.

"Thank you. I'm glad you two had a chance to meet. Too bad she's heading back to school in less than a week. I do miss her when she's gone. She's my baby. You'll have to meet the rest of my crew one of these days. But just because

I'm through training you, doesn't mean we can't be friends, Cassie. Fact is, I'd love for us to be friends.''

"I'd like that, too.''

Lottie took hold of her hand. "Good. Now, I brought you something I think you might need.'' She dug into her white shoulder bag.

"Oh, Lottie, you shouldn't have brought me anything.''

"It might be a gift,'' Lottie said, sliding a long rectangular box in front of her. "Then again, it might not.''

Stunned, Cassie peered down at a home pregnancy test.

"I've had five children, Cassie. I'd recognize the signs anywhere and, honey, you've got them all.''

Cassie lifted the box up slowly, her head spinning. "I can't be pregnant. I mean, the man I was with, uh, we used protection.''

"Well, it's better that you know for sure. One way or another, you should see a doctor. Since you've been here, you've been looking exhausted and your stomach isn't right, acting up all the time. Go ahead and try it.''

"Now?''

Lottie gave her an encouraging nod. "I'll be waiting right here.''

A short time later Cassie came out of the bathroom, her mind numb and her insides quaking. "It's positive,'' she announced to Lottie.

Lottie didn't miss a beat. She smiled brightly, her eyes gleaming. "Then it's a gift. What about the father, honey? How will he feel about this?''

The father? Cassie hadn't thought about the father. She was thinking about a new life growing inside of her and how all of this was possible. A baby? She'd been so sure this couldn't happen. They'd taken precautions that night.

"I'm amazed. I don't understand how this happened. Jake and I—"

"Jake?" Lottie's amber eyes lit with surprise. "Are you saying Jake is the father? *Our* Jake?"

Cassie slumped into the chair beside her. "Oh, Lottie." Cassie rested a protective hand on her belly, overwhelmed with the wonder of carrying a child. Jake's child. She was going to be a mother. Fear, awe and excitement replaced her disbelief. "It's a long story."

Lottie assured her with a smile, "I've got nothing but time, honey. Tell me."

Thirty minutes later, amid tears and chuckles and every emotion in between, Cassie had informed Lottie of the entire story. It felt good to confide in someone and Lottie had the kindest heart. She was a person Cassie could trust.

"Wow," Lottie said, sitting back in her chair.

"I know. My life hasn't been dull. I thought by moving here things would sort of even out. I thought life would get easier."

"Babies are blessings, Cassie. And who's to say your life won't just turn out wonderful."

Cassie frowned, unable her hide her concern and trepidation from her new friend.

Lottie sat straight up in the chair again. Sparkling with excitement, she announced, "I know what you need, honey. You need to get out and meet some new people. You need to get away from this ranch and get your mind off your troubles for one day." She dug back into her handbag, coming up with an invitation. "We're going to a shindig tomorrow night. It says right here, 'Lottie Fairchild and guest.' You're going to be my guest, honey. It's a party for Ted O'Hanley. He's turning the big 4-0 tomorrow and his father is throwing him a big old birthday bash. Say you'll come."

"Oh, Lottie, I don't know." Yet the more Cassie thought

about it, the more appealing the idea became. Maybe she
did need some time to clear out the cobwebs in her head.
"I'd…like to. I mean, I haven't really been off this ranch
much since I got here. But jeez, I just don't know. Besides,
what would I wear?"

Lottie grinned. "Shut down that computer. You're
through with work for the day. We're going shopping. We'll
find you just the right outfit."

"Shopping?" Cassie began to smile. Gosh, that sounded
like fun. Doing anything with Lottie would be fun. The
woman was a ball of fire, all sweet-natured energy and
gusto. And Lottie did have a point. Cassie needed a change
of scenery. She didn't want to think about Jake or the fact
that she'd have to tell him real soon that she was carrying
his child. "Okay, let's do it. Let's go shopping!"

Saturday evening Jake stood on the porch steps glancing
to his right, wondering what the dickens the two women
were up to. Even from this distance, fifty feet away from
the guest house, he could hear the sound of their cheerful
laughter. Lottie was decked out in her going-out clothes and
he couldn't miss Cassie's wild cinnamon hair, flowing
around her face, a mass of soft silk and waves. She wore a
beige Western dress that tied up the front with suede strings
and a pair of matching boots, looking every bit the part of
a ranching woman. When the women jumped into Lottie's
Blazer, Jake stepped off the porch and planted himself on
the road.

Lottie pulled up beside him. "Hi, Jake."

Jake leaned in, his gaze flowing from Lottie straight to
Cassie. She looked drop-dead gorgeous. "Ladies. Planning
on a big night?"

Cassie cast him a weak smile then turned her head to peer
out the window.

"We're heading to Ted's birthday bash. I figured it was time for Cassie to meet some of our neighbors. She hasn't been off the ranch much. She's due for some fun."

Jake nodded. "Well, have a good time."

The car ambled down the road as Jake climbed back up the steps to the porch. John T. was waiting for him. "What was that all about?"

"Lottie's taking Cassie to Ted O'Hanley's party."

John T. nodded and they both stared at Lottie's car as it made its way down the road toward the gates of the property.

"Isn't Ted's father newly widowed?" Jake asked.

"Yep. About a year now."

"He was always sweet on Lottie, wasn't he?"

John T. frowned and rubbed his jaw. "Bet Cassie'll stir up a lot of interest being new to the valley and all. Her dance card's sure to be filled."

Jake peered out, straight across the road. "I wasn't planning on going."

"Nah, me neither," John T. agreed.

A moment passed.

Jake slanted his father a look. "How long before you can be ready?"

"About twenty minutes."

Jake nodded. "Once we get there, it's every man for himself."

Eight

Cassie's mind whirled in ten different directions. She'd been introduced around by Lottie to nearly every one of the guests in the Knights of Columbus Hall. Her head had clicked off the numbers, realizing she'd met exactly fifty-three people so far. She'd already danced three times, had been asked out on a date by Ted's younger brother, Adam, and had been invited to an afternoon social by Mavis Brewer, an energetic woman who was running for city council. The way she'd been welcomed to Carson Valley by all of these friendly people warmed her heart and kept her mind off her troubles.

"Oh, Lottie, this is fun. I'm glad you invited me." They sat at a table off a ways from the festivities, sipping soda.

"Uh-oh, maybe you won't think so now," Lottie said with a crooked smile. "Trouble at two o'clock."

It took a moment for that to register. Cassie glanced in the direction of Lottie's concentration and realized exactly

what she'd meant. Cassie's good mood evaporated immediately upon seeing both Jake and John T. standing at the
entrance of the hall. "Double trouble, Lottie."

"They came together, now that's something. Those two
don't do a blasted thing together normally." Lottie reached
over to grab both of Cassie's hands. "At least it'll give you
a chance to talk to him, honey."

"I'll talk to John T. all night long."

Lottie's eyes twinkled. "You know darn well, darlin', I
was talking about Jake. You're gonna have to tell him."

Cassie knew that. She didn't think she'd have to face Jake
so soon though. She needed a little more time. Heavens, she
was just getting used to the idea of having a baby. It no
longer frightened her. In truth, Cassie had come full circle.
This morning, after a fitful night, Cassie realized the baby
for the miracle that it was. She'd always wanted children.
She'd just thought that love and marriage would have come
first. She had the "love" part down, but it couldn't be one-
sided. Cassie wanted more. She wasn't going to settle for
anything less. That much she knew already and she also
knew that she wasn't ready to tell Jake. "I know I have to
tell him, but not tonight."

"Whenever you feel it's right, honey. But you shouldn't
avoid him."

Cassie glanced at Jake. He was a hard man to avoid.
Standing there in new jeans, a black Western shirt and shiny
hat, looking absolutely breathtaking, he did just that. He
stole all of her breath. "Oh, Lottie."

Lottie released her hands and gestured with a tilt of her
head. "If you don't talk to him, about a dozen women will,
Cassie. They'll pounce on him like hounds on a fox."

Hounds on a fox? How appropriate, she thought.

"Okay, if he comes over here, I'll talk to him."

But Jake didn't come over. She felt his presence, his gaze

on her as he stood in a group of young cowboys, chatting away, sipping drinks, at the opposite end of the hall.

John T. had come over immediately. He'd talked with them awhile, had kicked up his heels with Lottie twice and had asked Cassie to dance, as well. She'd danced with Adam O'Hanley once more, who had persisted in asking her out again, then she danced with two other cowboys before excusing herself and heading to the rest room. Drained, tired and immensely annoyed that Jake hadn't bothered to come over to say hello, Cassie took a moment to splash water on her face. She fluffed waves that didn't really need fluffing, reapplied a bit of lip gloss, but nothing helped hide the lines of fatigue around her eyes.

Once she exited the rest room, she noted John T. and Lottie deep in conversation at the table. Cassie didn't want to interrupt such an intimate scene, so she walked over to the bar to get another soda.

Suddenly, Jake was beside her, leaning on the bar. He was close, enough for his shoulders to brush against her. "Having fun?" he asked.

"Yes. I have Lottie to thank for inviting me." She thanked the bartender for her root beer and turned to face him. "I'm meeting the nicest people."

"Including Adam O'Hanley?"

"Adam? How did you—"

"It's a small community." A tick worked in Jake's jaw. "News travels like wildfire, especially at a party like this. He struck out twice with you."

"I, uh, I'm not here looking for a date."

Jake's expression changed, his mouth twisting in a smug smile. "Unlike that night in Laughlin."

He would have to bring that up. "That was different. I was desperate that night."

"I remember. I remember that entire weekend, Cassie."

His voice softened to a velvety caress. "Having a hard time forgetting it."

She hadn't forgotten, either, but now there was much more to think about, such as the fact that she was carrying Jake's child as a result of the passion they'd shared that night. Cassie fanned her face with her hand. "I think I need some air."

She headed straight for the door. Once outside, fresh Nevada air hit her and she breathed in deeply. She leaned up against the side of the building surprised that Jake had followed her outside. Her announcement hadn't been an invitation to join her.

Jake removed the root beer from her hand, replacing it with a glass of ice-cold water. "Try this instead." He guided the glass to her lips and made sure she sipped it.

"Thanks. I got a little…breathless in there."

Jake took the water glass from her hand, set it down, then came up close, bracing his hands on the wall on both sides of her. Trapped by his surrounding presence, Cassie looked up into dark, hungry eyes. "I get breathless whenever I look at you, darlin'."

When Jake turned on the charm, she found herself hopelessly captivated. He stood close, brushing his body against the soft folds of her dress. "You look beautiful tonight, Cassie." He ran a finger down her cheek, the caress enough to make Cassie's heartbeat speed out of control. And when he leaned in, she didn't have the strength or the willpower to stop him. He brushed a kiss to her lips, softly at first, exquisitely, taking it slow, giving her time to make up her mind. And when she didn't protest, he pressed his body against hers, all hard lines and firm muscle swaying her to his will. He wrapped his arms around her, deepening the kiss, whispering words of encouragement. He parted her lips and drove his tongue deep, stroking her masterfully. Cassie's entire body trembled, from Jake's kiss, but also from sheer exhaustion.

Cassie wasn't up for this. She'd never experienced such highs and lows in her life. One minute she was a bundle of energy, then the next it was as though her legs wouldn't hold her upright another second. And she couldn't tell Jake why. She wasn't ready for him to learn the truth. ''I'm sorry,'' she said, shoving him away slightly. She wiped at her forehead and looked away. On a weary sigh she said, ''I think I need to go home.''

Jake hesitated. His eyes were on her, his gaze steady, measuring. He lifted her chin with a finger to turn her face his way. ''You really mean that, don't you? You're not feeling well.''

She nodded, banking her tears, hoping to keep Jake from guessing the truth. If only she could buy time the way one could buy a vowel on a television game show.

I'd like to buy another month, please.

But this wasn't a game and the only puzzle to solve was what she was going to do about Jake Griffin, the father of her child.

''Wait right here, honey.''

Jake took off and within two minutes he was back with keys in his hand. ''John T. will hitch a ride with Lottie. C'mon,'' he said, taking her hand and leading her to the parking lot. ''I'll drive you back to the ranch.''

''Jake,'' she said, wanting to protest, but Lottie and John T. were making headway. The last thing Cassie wanted to do was to interrupt their evening. ''Okay, it's probably for the best.''

Jake opened the truck door for her and she climbed in. Once Jake was seated behind the wheel, he turned to her with a wink. ''I really didn't want to go to that party, anyway.''

''Why did you, then?''

Jake didn't answer. Or was his silence enough of an answer? Cassie was too doggone tired to think about anything but resting her head on her pillow and letting sleep claim her.

The rumbling of the motor, the quiet darkness of the night and the cozy warmth inside the truck nearly lulled her to sleep. She'd close her eyes, only to open them and find Jake's questioning gaze on her. Cassie fought her fatigue and breathed a silent sigh of relief once they'd arrived at the ranch.

Jake walked her to the door. ''Are you sure you're all right?''

She stood on the porch, facing him. ''I'll manage. I can't wait to climb into bed.''

Jake took the key out of her hand and unlocked the door. ''That's exactly what you should do. Cassie, you're pale and you look so doggone exhausted. I'd tuck you in myself but that wouldn't work now, would it?''

Cassie shook her head slowly.

He blew out a sigh. ''Good night then. Get some rest.'' He leaned over and kissed her cheek and then was gone.

Cassie locked her door and within minutes she'd found the sleep she needed.

The next morning Jake came up right behind Lottie as she knocked on Cassie's door. ''Oh, Jake! I didn't see you. You nearly scared my hair into its natural color!''

''Sorry, Lottie. Just came to check on Cassie before I leave.'' He glanced down at the goodie basket in Lottie's hand. ''What's in the basket today? I'm heading for Oklahoma this morning. Sure could use some of your blueberry muffins to fill my belly.''

"Uh, no. Nothing like that in here." Lottie clung tight to her basket. "Just some things to make Cassie feel better."

Jake grinned. "Well, let me see. I sure bet there's something in there to make me feel better, too." Jake took the basket out of Lottie's hand, curious as to why she seemed so reluctant to let it go.

He unwrapped the toweling. "Crackers, ginger ale and what's this...a book?" Jake lifted the book out of the basket, reading, then rereading the title, until it sunk in. "'*The ABC's of Childbirth, a Pregnancy Guide.*'" Five smiling diaper-clad babies adorned the cover.

Jake stared at the book then lifted his gaze to Lottie. She had compassion in her eyes and a tinge of guilt.

Jake clenched his teeth. "Now it all makes sense." All of the clues had been right there in front of him, the bouts of fatigue, the fainting spells, and John T. had mentioned that Cassie had been sick to her stomach when she'd first arrived. Jake's mind whirled with incident after incident, leaving no room for doubt now. Cassie was pregnant.

"Jake?"

"I need to speak with Cassie, in private," he declared, his lips tight, his gut tighter. Temper flaring, he could barely see beyond the stunned fury he experienced.

"Yes, you two need to talk, but don't upset her, Jake. Give her time to explain."

The front door opened then and Cassie smiled at Lottie. "This is a surprise."

Jake made his presence known by stepping right next to Lottie.

"Oh, Jake." Cassie shot Lottie a questioning look.

"I'm sorry, honey," Lottie said. "I only came by to help."

"We need to talk, Cassie," he announced. "Alone."

Cassie's chin went up defiantly. "This isn't a good time, Jake."

"Damn right, it isn't. I'm heading out to Oklahoma today."

"Talk to him, honey," Lottie said with an encouraging tone and a quick smile. "I'll leave you two alone."

Cassie swallowed and nodded, moving away from the door, giving him entrance. Jake strode in and waited while Cassie said goodbye to Lottie and closed the door.

Cassie stood by the door, her green eyes wide with trepidation, her arms crossed around her middle. Jake flung the book on the sofa, the title and cover facing her, hard to be missed. "Lottie thought this might make good reading material."

Cassie peered at the book, mouthed something that looked like "Oh, no," then closed her eyes for a moment.

Impatient, Jake prodded her for a response. "When were you going to tell me?"

"I—I, uh, needed time to adjust to the idea."

"You should have told me straightaway. I had a right to know, dammit. How long have you known?" he asked, his temper simmering. He held it in check, barely.

"Just a few days. Lottie is the only one who knows. She guessed it before I even had a clue. I guess I figured it couldn't happen. We used protection."

Jake stared into Cassie's eyes, remembering. "It was a pretty wild night. Anything was possible."

He watched Cassie swallow down hard and lay a hand on her abdomen. She was carrying his child. Jake had a lump in his throat, too. He was going to be a father.

Jake began pacing, his mind whirling. He never wanted this. He never intended to father a child. Hell, after the bad example John T. set, and one failed marriage, Jake had to be a damn fool to think of raising a family of his own. But the fact remained, Cassie was carrying his baby. He had to make it right. He halted his pacing to stand right in front of her. "Okay, okay. Soon as I get Oklahoma out of the way, we'll get married. We'll do it up quick and simple. I'll be back next Monday."

"No, I don't think so," Cassie said instantly. She'd let Jake bully his way in here because she'd been caught off guard, but that was about to end. She brushed past him and strode into the kitchen. With surprisingly steady hands she poured herself a cup of decaf coffee and sat down at the kitchen table.

Jake followed her into the kitchen. With hands on hips, he loomed over her. "I'm not one for big weddings, but if that's what you want…"

Cassie tilted her head and peered up at him. "I don't want a big wedding. I don't want a wedding at all. I'm not going to marry you."

Jake's eyebrows rose and fell. His lips twitched. He blinked, taken completely aback; looking at her as if she'd spoken a foreign language he didn't comprehend. "What?"

Cassie turned her face away and sipped her coffee. She hated confrontations, but she knew she couldn't marry Jake. Jeez, even Rick had done a better job of proposing. But at least with Rick there was the idea of love behind the marriage proposal. Cassie knew without a doubt, Jake didn't love her. He didn't want to marry. She was nothing to him but an obligation.

Heavens, he'd just learned that he was going to be a father and how did he put it? As soon as he got back from Oklahoma he'd get the nasty business of marrying her *out of the way*.

Quick and simple.

Cassie couldn't make another mistake. Now that she had a baby to consider, she didn't want to make any hasty decisions. She knew the baby took priority, but marrying Jake wasn't the answer. He wasn't capable of loving her the way she wanted. He had an entire set of priorities that didn't include her. The rodeo, for one. And holding on to his bitterness toward his father, for another. Cassie had an uncanny feeling that somehow the two went hand in hand.

And most of all, Cassie refused to play second fiddle again.

"Thank you for the offer, but no thanks," Cassie repeated.

Jake came around the table to face her. With hands braced on the tabletop and arms rigid, he leaned in. "You're carrying my child, Cassie."

"Yes, I'm aware of that."

Nostrils flaring, his intense gaze pinned her down. "And you're refusing to marry me?"

"Yes. Yes, I am." She wouldn't allow Jake to intimidate her. Somehow, over the past month, Cassie had gained the strength she needed to stick to her resolve. She'd made herself a promise and was bound and determined to keep it. But oh, how wonderful it would have been if Jake's proposal had come out of love and commitment. How quickly she'd grab that brass ring and settle into life with him and their baby.

Jake straightened, his hands flying up in the air in a gesture of frustration. "I know what you're doing, Cassie. It's that crazy reasoning of yours. You're attracted to me, but that's a bad thing because you don't trust your instincts anymore. You don't want to get hurt again. Okay, I get that. But you have to get something, too. I'm not going to allow the baby—*my* baby—to be raised in a fatherless home. Children need two parents. They need to know they'll always have a roof over their head and food on the table. They need to know that when bad times hit, they have someone to turn to, someone who will always be there for them.''

"Jake, it's not as though you won't see the baby."

"Dammit, Cassie! That's not enough. I won't repeat the same pattern my father set. I won't abandon my child."

"You wouldn't be."

"The child needs a stable home life. The baby needs to have my name."

"The baby needs much more than that. And so do I."

Jake cursed then, taking time to breathe deeply. He stared at her, his gaze probing, searching. Quietly he asked, "What do you want, Cassie?"

Cassie stood and suddenly realized exactly what she wanted. She wanted it with an intensity that shook her to her core. She stared back at Jake, loving him, perhaps not a wise thing, but loving him all the same. With sadness in her heart, for Jake and all he'd gone through as a child, she spoke with clarity. "I want what you can't give me, Jake. Have a good trip."

Cassie headed to the bedroom and closed the door. She laid a hand on her abdomen and only when she heard the soft click of her front door, did she allow one sole tear to trickle down her cheek.

Nine

"I'll call you if I need anything. Yes, anything at all, I promise," Cassie said, twisting the phone cord in her fingers. Early morning sunlight brightened her kitchen and Cassie squinted, turning away to lean against the counter. "I love you, too, Brian. And tell Alicia not to worry about me, either. I'm getting the hang of this pregnancy thing."

Cassie hung up the phone and released a long sigh. Of course Brian was worried about her. Of course, both he and Alicia wanted her to return home, to Los Angeles. But oddly, Cassie felt more at home here, at the ranch with work she enjoyed and her new friendship with Lottie and John T. She'd tried to put it as delicately as possible that she didn't need Brian's help right now, just his moral support.

She'd thought Brian would have a coronary when she'd told him about her pregnancy. Brian put all the blame on Jake, accusing him of neglecting her, but Cassie had set him straight immediately. To Jake's credit, he'd tried to do the right thing by offering her marriage. And Cassie had tried to explain to Brian that a marriage without love and commitment would be no marriage at all. Brian hadn't been easy to convince, he'd been too busy being a protective brother. He probably still wasn't entirely certain that Cassie was doing the right thing, but Cassie was sure, and in the end, that's all that really mattered.

A minute later Cassie stood facing John T. at her front door. He held a long, gold-foil flower box in his arms. "Did I miss your birthday?"

"Uh, no. That's not for several more months." Cassie let him in and accepted the box he handed her.

"They were delivered to the main house. Thought you'd like to have them fresh."

Cassie set the box down on the kitchen table and untied a crimson bow, opening the lid to an array of the most beautiful long-stemmed burnt-orange roses Cassie had ever seen before. Their color appeared unnatural for roses, the hue reminding her of cinnamon and honey. "Oh, these are amazing."

She fingered the petals, aware of John T.'s curious stare. She couldn't blame him. She was pretty curious, too. She found a card tucked into the stems and lifted it up to read it silently. "The color reminds me of your hair. Until Monday."

Emotion coiled tight in her stomach. She held back silly tears. Pregnancy had a way of blowing every slight sensation a woman felt into something wildly glorious or hideously monstrous. Cassie was certain she felt an equal measure of both right now. There were no words of endearment on the card, not even a signature, but Cassie knew intuitively that Jake Griffin rarely, if ever, sent flowers to a woman.

John T. waited patiently for an explanation. She wished

she didn't have to explain the roses to him, but he'd been kind to deliver them personally and to ignore his questioning look would be rude. "They're from Jake."

John T. blinked. "Jake? My son, Jake?"

Cassie chuckled, releasing a wave of emotion that she'd bottled up inside. John T.'s expression, the look on his face, mirrored her surprise. "Yes," she said, smiling now, "Jake sent them."

John T. stared down at the box filled with roses. "Well, if that don't beat all."

Cassie wouldn't explain about the baby to John T., believing it was Jake's place to tell his father if he hadn't already guessed. According to Lottie, Cassie's symptoms were classic and quite obvious to anyone who'd ever had a child of their own.

She put the roses in a water-filled vase, aware of John T.'s gaze on her. His eagle eyes appeared darker, the sharpness blunted, and a clouded expression seemed to fall on his face. She looked up from the vase she'd just placed on the kitchen table, wondering about his mood.

"I've got business in town today. There're some people you ought to meet. I'd like you to join me."

Cassie spent the remainder of the morning with John T., meeting his banker, being introduced to the mayor and having a pleasant lunch in the oldest restaurant in Carson City, a barbecue place that claimed the best ribs in the county. Cassie had to agree, they'd been wonderful. She'd been especially grateful her stomach had cooperated.

Yet there had been something odd about John T. today, his usual gruffness replaced by something subtle, a mellow attitude almost bordering on sadness. It was just a feeling Cassie had, and as he'd driven home, asking if she'd mind taking a slight detour, Cassie knew her intuition had been right on. They pulled into a cemetery. When they got out of the car and walked to a marked grave, Cassie had known whose name she'd see on the headstone.

"It's John Junior's birthday today. He would have been twenty-seven." John T. slanted her a somber look and sorrow filled her heart. "I shouldn't have let him take the boat out that day. He wasn't ready."

Cassie swallowed hard. Gently she touched his arm. "You couldn't have known."

He smiled sadly. "His mother was against it. She'd been right, and I'll go to my grave regretting that decision. I think I indulged that boy too much out of guilt over my other son, the one I didn't acknowledge. I had no idea that Jake's mother passed away when he was just five years old. I really didn't. I'd lost contact with Isabella. It's the way she wanted it, but it was easier for me, too, I'll admit. I didn't have to explain a love affair and an illegitimate child to my wife. After John's death I did everything I could to find Jake, and when I did and brought him back here, I wanted to make things right with him. But I'd been too late. He wouldn't allow me to be his father." He stopped briefly, staring intently at the grave, and Cassie noticed his body trembling. He shook his head with sorrow. "In a sense, I lost both my boys."

Cassie reached out to take his hand, looking into his eyes. "I don't think you've lost Jake. I think once he becomes a father, he'll be more understanding."

He flinched, doubt creeping into his expression. "I don't know if I'll live to see the day."

Cassie heard the anguish in his voice and it pained her greatly. This proud and cantankerous man rarely opened his heart to anyone. He'd held his heartache in for years, using it as a shield perhaps, not unlike Jake. For him to confide in her and to bring her to his son's grave, meant a great deal to Cassie. At that moment she made up her mind to tell John T. the truth. He'd find out soon enough, anyway, and today of all days, the man needed to hear good news. Babies had a way of giving people hope. "Jake's going to be a father sooner than you think." She pressed her hand to her stomach, her mind calculating the exact amount of days, almost to the minute, but she didn't bore him with the details. "I'd say in less than seven and a half months."

John T.'s sad expression changed instantly. He peered down at her hand splayed across her belly. Surprise registered, a kind of stunned amazement, then once he regrouped he took her hand and led her to a wrought-iron bench on the grounds. "Want to tell me about it?"

Cassie left out the torrid details, but she did speak candidly with John T. about her life and past mistakes, how she met up with Jake at the rodeo and how much she wanted to do the right thing for the baby. He seemed to understand, but she wasn't quite sure he agreed with her decision not to marry Jake.

"He wants to marry me out of obligation. He doesn't love me. I don't think that's any way to raise a child, in a loveless home."

"Are you saying you don't love my son?" John T.'s eyes softened on hers and Cassie knew he wasn't pressuring her, only trying to get at the truth.

"I'm saying it might be a big mistake marrying him. I don't want to be hurt again."

John T. sighed, leaning back against the seat. They'd been talking for a long time, sharing confidences with brutal honesty. "My son is a stubborn one, but I think we both know he's worth the trouble."

Cassie smiled softly. John T. was right. Jake was a woman's best kind of trouble. She was dreadfully in love with him, but set on protecting herself. He'd built up great walls of defense, shutting people out, and Cassie knew until he learned how to open up and forgive, she'd never have his love.

"Yes, he's worth the trouble. But I won't play second fiddle again so I guess we're at a stalemate right now." Cassie couldn't bring herself to say that she and the baby deserved to be loved. That she'd dreamed about one day having a family, a husband who loved her and a child to adore, but circumstances had always gotten in the way. Cassie couldn't resign herself to anything less. She'd reached a plateau in her life and wouldn't back down. If anything, she would rise up even higher and fight like mad not to go tumbling downward.

John T. grinned. "You're a tough cookie, Cassie Munroe. Jake's gotta have rocks in his head not to fall in love with you." He leaned over and kissed her cheek, then stood, offering her his hand. "C'mon, let's get my grandchild home. I bet his mama is tired."

A streaming ray of sunshine slanting in from her window woke Cassie from a sound sleep. She let out a tiny groan of dismay. Mornings were tough. She'd overcome her bouts of queasiness, thankfully, but getting out of bed seemed like a huge endeavor lately. No matter how much she slept at night, she'd always wake up feeling as though she hadn't slept at all.

But it was Monday morning and she had a pile of work on her desk, so she pressed herself up, washed her face and headed to the kitchen to make a pot of decaf. Halfway there, she stopped up short, catching her breath when she realized she was not alone. Her heart hammered with dread as she heard sounds coming from the living room. Slowly she walked in to investigate, blaming an overactive imagination. She'd always felt safe living at the ranch.

When she spotted him asleep on her couch, she gasped out loud. "Jake?"

One eye opened lazily.

"What are you doing here?" With hands on hips, she gazed down, not caring that her raised voice made the sleepy man jump.

He opened both eyes now, squinted up at her, then smiled, a lazy sort of smile that could charm the pants off of...well, her. Darn him. Her irritation ebbing, she shook her head. "Let me guess, you still have the key to the house."

"Good morning to you, too, darlin'," he said, his eyes adjusting to the morning light. Sprawled out on his back on the sofa, wearing nothing but faded jeans, unsnapped at the waist, he stretched and scratched his chest, his fingers splaying through scattered coils of hair.

Cassie's toes curled. The man gave new meaning to the word seductive.

"I drove straight through. Got in very early this morning. I wanted to see you."

"Jake, you can't crash on my sofa anytime you want."

"Would you rather I'd joined you, in bed? I sure have to admit, it was tempting." He focused on her nightclothes, a soft pink tank top and matching cotton shorts. His expression left no room for doubt what would have happened if he shared her bed.

"Jake," Cassie said, exasperated. The man knew how to turn her on, big time, but she fought the lusty images flashing in her head. She couldn't fall victim to him again. And where had all this charm come from, especially so early in the morning? Cassie felt like the Wicked Witch of the West until she had her first cup of coffee.

Alert now, and sitting up, she noted his gaze traveling over her body and resting solely on her abdomen, on the baby.

"How are you?" he asked.

"I'm fine, really."

"No more dizzy spells?"

"No, I'm over all that. I just tire more easily now, but that should pass soon, too."

"That's good."

He stood and stretched again. Cassie groaned silently, watching the fluid play of muscles tightening across his chest. She couldn't bring herself to tear her gaze away. She'd missed him.

"I'll fix us breakfast," he said.

Cassie headed to the kitchen. If the man wanted to cook for her, who was she to deny him that privilege? Since her bouts of queasiness had diminished, she found herself more often than not, famished. "Two eggs, over easy, bacon and toast, lathered in butter and orange juice, please."

He grinned devilishly. "I see you've gotten your appetite back."

"I'm eating for two now."

After an astonishingly good breakfast, Cassie carried the dishes to the sink. She began to load the dishwasher when a thought struck her. "I'd like you to return the house key," she said firmly, but she couldn't turn to meet his eyes. This was, after all, his home and he'd been gracious enough not to send her packing. She knew John T.'s ploy wouldn't have stopped Jake from reclaiming his home if he'd really wanted it. But he'd made the sacrifice for her. He was living in the main house with his father, a place he'd rather not be. The slight tinge of guilt she felt made her uneasy.

Jake came up from behind. He wrapped his arms around her waist and brought his body close, his groin pressing into her backside. He spoke softly in her ear. "Okay, but it's gonna cost you."

Her toes curled again and fiery heat shot through her. She

should just melt into him and be done with it. Whatever he had in mind would probably be too high a price. But Cassie couldn't have the sexy man traipsing into her house at all hours, playing havoc with her heart and mind.

She froze, her hands braced against the edge of the counter. Swallowing hard, she ventured, ''What…what do you want?''

His arms tightened around her and he kissed her throat, his tongue coming out to moisten the skin just behind her ear. Her skin prickled and an unwelcome tightness assailed her body. His warm breath across her throat and the faint scent of spicy aftershave reeled her senses. Then she found herself being turned in his arms. He stared at her lips. ''You know what I want, but for now I'll settle for this.''

His mouth claimed hers with urgent need, a tender kiss that escalated with each second that passed. Cassie was unable to stop it, to stop him from rekindling fiery passion that threatened like a live wire skittering out of control. His tongue brushed her lips, tasting her, pressing her, and she opened for him. Electricity filled the warm, sunlit room. Her heart pounded, her bones melted as Jake worked his magic with a demanding mouth, strong embrace and the hard beckoning call of his body.

Breathless, Cassie came up for air. She gazed into Jake's dark, smoldering and all too knowing eyes.

Backing up a step, he allowed her room to breathe. Then he opened her palm and placed something in her hand. The key.

''It's all yours, sweetheart. But don't think you'll be able to lock me out.''

He kissed her one last time then was gone.

Cassie stood there trembling.

She was trying with all of her heart to do just that.

To lock him out.

* * *

The next evening, just as Cassie was ready to toss a salad and throw a frozen pizza in the oven, the soft roar of an engine shutting down and the slamming of a car door, caught her attention. She peered out the kitchen window to find Jake with arms loaded, climbing up her steps. She closed her eyes and counted to ten. It didn't help. The knock came all too soon. She needed more time to brace herself for Jake's onslaught.

"Hi," she said, coming to the door. All too suddenly she became aware of her appearance. She'd thrown on an old pair of ripped-at-the-knee gray sweats and a white T-shirt, planning on slumming tonight in front of the television set. And she hadn't done a thing to her hair since applying a thick layer of mousse after her shower this morning. The auburn strands took on that stringy wet look—a perfect example of a bad hair day, the "before" style in a "before and after" demonstration.

Jake grinned, taking all of her in. "Cute, Cassie. I brought dinner and a movie." He peeked inside. "You haven't eaten, have you?"

"I, uh," she began, thinking about the rock-solid frozen pizza she was hoping would develop miraculously into a gourmet meal with a little heat and loving care. "No. But something sure smells good. What's in the bag?"

He winked. "Let me in and I'll show you."

The delicious aroma wafting in the air was far too tempting for Cassie to turn away. And Jake...well, turning him away was getting to be an arduous, nearly impossible task. How could she deny her heart and protect it at the same time?

But whatever was in that bag swayed her resolve. She was famished and hockey-puck pizza just wouldn't win out tonight. She let him in and followed him to the kitchen. He

began placing round aluminum dishes on the table, the scent
of fresh, buttery garlic hit her smack between the eyes.

"Angel-hair pasta with shrimp," he offered, lifting one
lid then the other. "Or chicken. I wasn't sure which you'd
prefer. We have both. There's antipasto salad, garlic bread
and lemon-raspberry cheesecake for dessert."

"Oh, it all sounds wonderful. I didn't know you liked
Italian food."

"Hey," he said, feigning offense, "we cowboys don't
just eat pork and beans, you know."

Cassie reached for plates and utensils, handing them to
him to set out on the table while she opted for apple juice
for her and beer for him from the refrigerator. But she
stopped up short as she closed the refrigerator door. The
domestic scene; Jake scattering plates on the table as they
worked together to set up the meal and his ability to know
exactly what she seemed to need, when she needed it, all
struck her with painful clarity. He wasn't here for the right
reasons. He'd come to slowly seduce her, to bend her to his
will and to make her agree to a marriage she knew wouldn't
work. She'd let her grumbling stomach make a decision, but
would her aching heart pay the price? He turned to her and
immediately noted the concern on her face. She wasn't good
at hiding her emotions, but maybe tonight that was a good
thing. She needed to clear the air.

"Cassie?"

"What are we doing here, Jake?"

He approached her slowly, taking the bottles from her
hands and setting them on the counter, his gaze never leaving her face. "We're having dinner, darlin', and then we'll
catch a movie. It's not a chick flick, but I hear it's pretty
good." His smile was meant to reassure, but it had the opposite effect, making her more wary, more cautious of what
might develop this evening. She wanted Jake. She couldn't

deny that and when he turned on the charm, he was positively irresistible.

"You should have called first."

"Probably," he admitted honestly, "but I'm leaving tomorrow for five days and I wanted to spend time with you tonight."

He was leaving again?

"Where are you going?" she asked, keeping trepidation out of her voice. It was best that they have time apart, so why did she hate the fact that he could pick up and leave so readily? From what she understood, he'd been doing it for years, using Anderson Ranch as his stopping place—somewhere to hang his hat when nowhere else was available. It was as though he had no ties or commitment to the ranch even though he had family here and friends. If he couldn't commit to his home, how could he commit to her?

"Arizona. Suzette and some of her college friends are coming down for the rodeo."

Blood drained from her face. She smiled, but if Jake had even an ounce of male perception, he'd read her thoughts and understand the falsity of her smile. "How nice."

She tried to brush past him to busy herself at the kitchen table, but he blocked her with a broad, unyielding body. He pinned her with a dark, earnest gaze. "She's like a sister to me, darlin'."

She knew that. Lottie and John T. both had told her as much. Her jealousy was unfounded and totally irrational. She blamed the pregnancy on her unreasonable assumptions. She looked away uncomfortably. "It's none of my business, anyway."

Jake put a finger under her chin and lifted gently, making her peer directly into his eyes. "It is your business. I'm not asking her to marry me. I'm asking you. She's not carrying my child. You are."

Cassie blinked. Another proposal from Jake?

Her first thought was that he'd better be a darn good rodeo rider because he certainly wouldn't win any championships in the gallantry department. And with dawning clarity, Cassie understood from what wasn't in Jake's proposal. Again she was reminded of his reasons for marrying her, which had nothing to do with the true conventions of marriage. No love. No real commitment. She did believe he'd make a good father, though, and she wouldn't deny him that right. But entering into a union that was one-sided, would be torture for her, misery for him and in the end the baby would suffer most.

She sighed. "I haven't changed my mind."

"I know, but I'm working on that."

As a true competitor, he probably relished the challenge she posed. But Cassie couldn't back down. This was too important. "You're not planning on sleeping here, are you?"

Jake reached out to toy with a strand of her hair, curling one unruly tress around his finger. His gaze swept over her face, his smile devilish. "I'm always *planning* on sleeping with you. But I promise I won't stay over. Unless…"

"Not a chance, cowboy," she said hurriedly.

Jake didn't take her rejection to heart. Instead they ate their meal then settled in for an evening in front of the television. Jake took the bigger sofa and Cassie got comfortable on the love seat. Both ate mouth-watering cheesecake while watching the DVD he'd brought over. He seemed enthralled with the action of Mel Gibson's latest war movie. With legs sprawled out in front of him, Jake sat slouched down, his dark hair curling against the collar of a rather worn chambray work shirt. Rarely had Cassie seen him so relaxed.

She wondered about his life, how he'd gotten to this point

with so much controlled anger and hostility toward his only living relative. She knew he barely tolerated John T. and that most likely the man had deserved some of Jake's wrath. But there came a time to forgive and Cassie wondered if Jake had it in his heart to give his father a second chance. Jake caught her staring at him and she immediately turned her attention back to the movie.

An hour later when the movie ended, true to his word, Jake stood to leave. Cassie thanked him for the meal and walked him outside. The air was warm but there was enough of a refreshingly cool breeze to lift her hair and tussle the strands, the windblown look a definite improvement, she thought. The faint sound of wind chimes from one of the outer buildings drifted out, a harmonious tinkling that soothed, a subtle awakening in the dark quiet night.

"I'll be back late Sunday night."

Cassie nodded, her lips pressed tight. She'd stopped herself from inviting him over when he returned. She didn't want to send him mixed messages. Being in close contact with Jake wouldn't make her task any easier. She knew his intentions and knew he'd do whatever he could to break down her defenses. But it was *his* defenses, the barrier he'd positioned around his heart, that was the real problem.

Sadly, Cassie understood too well that Jake might never allow himself to feel again. He might never know the joy of true and honest love, the no-strings-attached kind of love that broke down all defenses, tore down all obstacles and left you vulnerable, with only your faith and trust to hold you up and protect you.

"I'll miss you, Cassie," he said softly.

Her heart squeezed tight. The dull, numbing ache spread itself out until she felt hollow inside. She believed him. She'd miss him, too. When they weren't entirely at odds, they were good together, but it wasn't enough. Cassie needed more than benign companionship from the man she loved. "Have a safe trip, Jake."

Jake stepped closer.

Cassie took a step back.

"Don't be afraid of me," he said, searching her eyes. He took her into an embrace, his arms winding around her waist and the warmth of his touch seeping into her skin.

Cassie lifted her chin. She wouldn't show fear. She could stand up to Jake and come out the winner. "I'm not afraid."

He smiled, bent his head and kissed her gently on the lips. "Good night, Cassie."

Then he wrapped a hand around her abdomen, lifting her shirt to make small sweet circles on her bare skin. His fingertips lightly brushed over her belly where their child grew. He smiled again, staring down. "Good night, little baby."

Cassie stood on the porch long minutes after he was gone, hugging the post, holding on for dear life and realizing she hadn't come out the winner tonight. Jake's sweet approach, his soft words to his child and the adoring look in his eyes had completely defeated her. No longer able to bank her tears, she let them flow.

Ten

"**I** don't know how much longer I can live here," Cassie said, sipping her lemonade, thinking out loud. Lottie jerked her head up, her gaze softening as she came to sit down next to her.

Lottie had been a godsend, a blessing in the guise of a woman who had befriended her, given her advice and consoled her whenever she needed a lift. She'd taken her to see a doctor in town today, and Cassie had come away with a clean bill of health. Both baby and mommy were doing fine. In seven months the baby would be born. Seven months seemed like an eternity to her. She didn't know how she could continue to live at the ranch with Jake applying slow and steady pressure to marry him.

They sat by a small lake ten miles outside of town, tossing remnants of the lunch they'd bought to the jays, watching the cornflower-blue birds nip away at the crumbs.

"Is it Jake?" Lottie asked, a knowing glint in her eyes.

She nodded and let go a breathy sigh. "He's doing all the right things. He sent me flowers the other day. Did I tell you that? And he comes over to spend time with me. I guess you could say he's courting me in his own way, when he's in town."

"But?"

"But, I know it's his way of winning me over. He wants to marry me for the baby's sake."

"And you want more, right?"

"Right. Oh, Lottie, I don't know what to do. Sometimes I think I'm being unfair to him. But I have a bad history with men and things never seem to work out. I've learned my lesson. I don't just want more…I want it all, the whole package. I don't think Jake is capable of that. But when I'm with him, I can't think straight. He makes me crazy sometimes."

Cassie flung a piece of bread out onto the grassy bank, watching three birds race toward it. "My brother Brian wants me to move back home. Ironically, my ex-fiancé, who was also Brian's partner, has dissolved their partnership. He's branched out on his own. Brian offered me that position as his equal partner. My big brother needs me right now. And I'm thinking that maybe it might be best for the baby and me if I did leave."

Lottie scooted closer, her blue eyes resting softly on Cassie. "You're deeply in love with Jake and you're afraid he'll never be able to return your love. You think putting distance between you will protect your heart."

Lottie understood. It was as if she had read Cassie's heart. And then it hit Cassie with sudden clear impact that Lottie had been in the same position. She'd been in love, and when that love hadn't been returned, she'd moved on. "You understand."

"I'm living it, honey." She winked. "And I'll tell you

honestly, it is easier when you don't have to see him every day and wonder why the heck you stayed around so long. So, yes, I do understand. But you haven't put in the time that I have. I can't fault you, though. It's hard loving and not being loved in return.''

''John T. cares for you, Lottie. I thought you two were making headway.''

''He's an exasperating man, Cassie. And I know he cares, but drawing that man out was like pouring cold molasses on dry toast—not worth the wait. So I finally moved on. And I was having a really good time, until he started doing things.''

''Doing things?'' Cassie's mind reeled. This conversation was a great distraction and a way to ease tension. ''What kind of things, exactly?''

''Why, the man sent me roses! Imagine, after some twenty years, he sent me my first bouquet of roses and now I know why. He must have gotten the idea from Jake!''

Cassie burst out laughing. ''You're probably right. The flowers Jake sent had been delivered to the main house, so John T. brought them over and he had the strangest look on his face, like maybe he'd just gotten a clue.''

Lottie's face beamed. ''A real quick learner.''

They chuckled again and Cassie felt a little better after their talk. Lottie hadn't pressured her to stay because she'd been in the same predicament. She truly did understand how Cassie felt about Jake.

''So tell me, what other things is John T. up to?''

''Well, just the other day he called to invite me to the chamber of commerce dinner, but I had to refuse. I had plans to spend the evening with my oldest son and his children. The man hates not getting his way. He got grouchy on the phone with me so I hung up on him.''

''You didn't!''

"I did and I'd do it again. I took his gruff ways when I worked for him, but I don't have to anymore. He has to learn how to treat a woman. I think I'm making him a little crazy."

Cassie grinned. "Why's that?"

"Because not five minutes later he called back to apologize. If you know anything about John T., you know he rarely apologizes to anyone, about anything. But he was very sweet when he called so I agreed to go out to dinner with him next week."

"That's great, Lottie. Really, really great."

"Yeah, I guess. It's taken twenty years for the molasses to heat up, honey. I haven't got that much time left."

Twenty years? Cassie didn't know if she could hold out for the next few months. Jake would be home in a few days. She'd have to give Brian's offer a great deal of thought and hope that she'd make the right decision, one that was best for everyone.

Jake sat in John T.'s study, leaning back in the chair, one booted foot crossed over the other in a casual position he didn't feel at the moment. He'd come home too late last night to visit Cassie, so he'd bounded out of bed first thing this morning, showered and dressed quickly and headed down the stairs, eager to see her this morning. He'd almost made it out the door when John T.'s booming voice had stopped him, calling him to the older man's office.

Jake tapped out a hasty rhythm on the arm of the chair, staring at John T., but his mind was on Cassie and how much he'd missed her these past five days. He'd found himself thinking about her often while he was away, thoughts of her messing up his concentration, making for less than perfect practice runs with Shadow. His roping skills had suffered, as well. It had taken supreme effort on his part to stay focused during the actual roping event and even at that, he'd battled to come in second place.

"I'm going to need your help around here, son," John T. stated plainly. "Toby is out of commission for a few days with a sprained wrist and a few of the boys are out sick. Work's been piling up. We could use your skills here."

Jake scrubbed his jaw, wondering if this was just another of John T.'s ploys to keep him home for a spell. And it never thrilled him when John T. called him *son*. He'd always known that he was John T.'s son by default only. His father used that term only when he needed something from Jake. "I'm heading out again next week, but I'll pitch in until then."

"That'll do fine," John T. said with authority. Jake hated sitting in his study facing off with the stern man as if he were a schoolboy who'd been summoned to the principal's office. Hell, he'd had enough of those real-life memories to clog his head for years to come.

Anxious to leave the house and find Cassie, Jake made a move to rise. "Not so fast. There's something else I want to discuss with you."

Jake lowered his body down again and sighed, causing John T. to lift his graying brows. "What else?"

"Your birthday's coming up soon."

Jake scoffed. He didn't like being reminded of his birthday. It had never been a happy occasion for him. As a young boy he had one vague memory of cake and candles, of delight and laughter, of his attempts to blow out tapering flames and of the only gift he'd remembered receiving from his mother—a watercolor she'd painted of a little boy sitting atop a gray mare, his face infused with joy, amid a mountain backdrop. Jake had kept that picture with him always. It was almost as though his mother had known that one day he'd end up here at Anderson Ranch, or was it just wishful thinking on a hope-filled young woman's part? Jake had surmised that must have been his fifth birthday because it was the last happy memory he'd had, faint as it was, of his mother. "I don't do birthdays, John T. You know that."

"Well, it's time, don't you think? I'd like to throw a little party. I'd like us to celebrate as a family."

"No. I don't think so." His face set, Jake wanted to leave no room for doubt. He had no need for a strained celebration, no need for John T.'s brand of family. It was too late for those things.

"Things are different now, Jake," John T. persisted. "You're going to be a father."

Jake jerked his head up. "You know?"

His father nodded, his voice taking on a somber edge. "Cassie told me the other day. Good thing, too, because I doubt I'd have heard it anytime soon from you."

Jake stood and began pacing. He glanced out the window, his anger swallowing him up, blinding him from seeing anything but Cassie's constant rejection. Hell, he didn't know what the woman wanted. He braced his hands on the back of the leather chair and leaned in. "We have some things to work out. I suppose she told you that I've asked her to marry me and she refused. I'll be damned if I'm going to let that woman walk out of my life. I plan on raising my child."

John T. nodded, his eagle-sharp eyes following his every move.

"There's not much else to say, is there?" Jake couldn't keep the bitterness out of his tone. On the one hand, he was furious with Cassie for refusing his proposal and denying him a future with his child. But on the other hand, he couldn't wait to see her. Couldn't wait to gaze into those big green eyes. Or kiss the sass right off that pouty little mouth of hers. Thoughts of her clouded his mind, messing with his focus and concentration.

"There is, if you're in love with her, son."

Jake huffed out a breath. Love? He wasn't sure he knew that emotion. He'd thought he was in love once, but that relationship had ended with a quick divorce. He knew he wanted Cassie, desired her in a way that made him crazy. He wanted to make love to her, and if she ever agreed to marry him, visions of long, slow, seductive nights danced in his head. And he wanted his child. He wanted to be the kind of father John T. hadn't been. He wanted to be there for his child at every turn, to let him know he wasn't alone. He wanted his child to have what Jake had never had—his father's name.

When Jake gave him no answer, John T. grimaced, a look of frustration sweeping across his features. "Hell, I wish I knew what to tell you. But I'm the last man to give advice regarding women. At least, think about the birthday celebration, son."

Son? There it was again. "I don't have to think about it, John T. My answer is no." Jake strode to the door. "I have work to do."

Jake slammed the door, heading for the guest house, but the carefree sound of Cassie's laughter had him turning toward the stables. It didn't take him long to spot her, surrounded by four ranch hands, the whole group looking extremely happy with themselves.

Jake's gut clenched. One of the men had taken his hat off and plopped it on Cassie's head. She was wearing denim today, a short skirt and Western boots. In that getup, Cassie looked as though she truly belonged here, as if she were made to live at the ranch. Her appearance stirred his blood but made it boil, too. Was she deliberately flirting with the hands, trying to find a man she wasn't attracted to, someone she'd feel safe with, someone she could trust with her heart? Irrational as it seemed, Jake couldn't get the notion out of his head.

He sidled up next to her and laced his arm around her waist. Without giving her notice, he pulled her close so that her waist brushed against him and he kissed her soundly on the lips. Her sweet, startled taste rattled his brain. "Good morning, darlin'. Did you miss me?"

Jake ignored Cassie's flaming face. He glanced at all four men, making eye contact with each one individually. Their shock at his actions didn't surprise him. Other than his short-lived marriage, Jake had never brought a woman to the ranch before, and he doubted the men knew his history with Cassie. It was about time he staked his claim. "Morning, boys."

They grumbled perfunctory greetings in return.

"John T. tells me we're shorthanded today. I'm taking over Toby's duties until he gets back."

One by one, the men tipped their hats to Cassie and said their goodbyes. Jake lifted the hat off her head and handed it back to the youngest of the crew, a cowboy named Nate. "Here you go," he said, "best to keep this on your own head."

"Yes, sir." Nate blushed and took off to do his chores.

Jake turned to Cassie, her face a mass of emotion he didn't want to consider. He returned her look with one equally as quelling. "Well, you didn't answer my question. Did you miss me?"

Cassie glared at Jake, too irritated to give him an answer. She'd been happy to see him, for about half a second, until he'd mortified her with that kiss, the deliberate message he sent to the ranch hands sounding loud and clear.

She turned on her heel and swiftly headed for the guest house.

Jake followed her. "Dammit, Cassie. Slow down."

"Go away, Jake." She kept on walking.

"I'm not going away. I'm staying, so you might as well talk to me."

"You'll be going away soon enough. You always do."

"Hey," Jake said, taking her arm gently, stopping her stride and turning her to face him. "You did miss me."

Cassie paused to look deep into his dark eyes. Ranch sounds surrounded her; a distant hammering from the barn area, horses whinnying out of unison and truck motors revving up. Dust swirled around, coloring the air a hazy reddish-brown only to be lifted away by a light wind as the Nevada sun beat down with simmering morning heat. Cassie sighed, not ready for this confrontation. Up until his appearance this morning, she'd been having a pleasant day. "You had no right to kiss me that way, Jake. I was working on the payroll and had some questions for the boys. We were having a nice conversation until you showed up."

"You're going to be my wife," he stated without hesitation. "No sense hiding it."

"I've never agreed to that, Jake. You can't bully me into marriage."

Jake lips went tight. He spoke with deliberation, a hard and ruthless edge to his voice. "You talk about rights? Well, what about mine? That's my baby growing in your belly. I have a right to raise my own child. I have a right to see him grow, watch him conquer big and small things alike. What's the problem, Cassie? You live here at the ranch. You work here. What's wrong with sharing a marriage bed? We do that well enough. What's wrong with getting married?"

"Oh, Jake." Cassie sighed deeply. "There's nothing right about us getting married. The reasons should be clear."

"Nothing's clear," he admitted. "In fact, whenever I look at you, my mind muddies up real thick."

Cassie stared at him, seeing him for the man he truly was, a drop-dead handsome cowboy whom she loved with unwelcome pain. She didn't have to ask him if he loved her. Her pride wouldn't allow it, anyway. But sadly she knew the truth. He was a man incapable of love. "I have to go."

"Hold up a sec," Jake said. "Don't go just yet."

"Why?"

"There's something I want to show you. Something you didn't get to see on the nickel tour a while back. I'm taking over the ranch superintendent's duties until Toby can get back and I want to show you what this ranch is really all about. Up on the north pasture."

His enthusiasm, the light in his eyes, the eager change in his voice, had Cassie curious. She'd never seen Jake respond with such animation before. Yet the north pasture was quite a long way away. She didn't know if she trusted herself with Jake all alone up there.

"Come on, Cassie. Say you'll go. I'll have you back here in an hour or two. We'll take the truck up there. I don't want to risk you on a horse."

His warm gaze fell on her belly and Cassie's heart softened. She found herself wanting to go, wanting to see just what Jake had to show her. She had missed him and since his mood had changed she found herself ready to spend time with him, but she needed to set rules to preserve her own sanity. "I'll go on one condition. You have to promise there'll be no talk of pressuring me into marrying you. The subject is off-limits."

Jake smiled and nodded. "I promise." He took her in his arms, pulling her close, and brought his lips down, kissing her with scorching heat. Cassie's body responded immediately, edging its way closer to him, her lips tingling, her body trembling. She moaned, a little sound that had Jake deepening the kiss, slanting over her lips with sweet, tortuous pressure. The kiss lasted longer than it should, considering that they stood right in the middle of the road, in sight of anyone who had a mind to watch.

When Cassie came to her senses, she backed away, ending the kiss and blinking, her fingers going to her ravaged lips. "And...and no more of that...either."

Jake only smiled and took her hand. "I figured as much. C'mon."

Twenty minutes later Cassie stood next to Jake on a rise, under the shadow of one of the few aging oaks on the north end of the land. They looked out at a herd of horses that made up the bulk of Anderson Ranch's wealth.

"Aren't they something?" Jake asked, his tone filled with awe.

The horses grazed peacefully, but there was wildness about them, a keen look in their eyes that even a rookie rancher like Cassie could recognize. "All of these are bucking horses?"

"Yep, every single one. They get exercised five days a week and we put them on a special diet to strengthen their bodies. They run the length of the pasture and back many times. Notice their legs—see the thick muscle there? That's to keep them strong when they buck."

"What makes them buck?" Cassie asked, never giving the idea any thought. Of course, she'd only been to one rodeo. "Their spirit mostly. There're a small percentage of animals that can't ever be tamed. They want no part of it and will fight against being broken with everything they've got. They've got no need for the sedate life most ranch horses enjoy. They are God's creatures kept entirely the way He made them." Jake pointed one out.

"See that one over there, the paint with the brown and

white markings? That's Texas Thunder. He comes from a long line of bucking horses. His mama was famous and his daddy bucked for over fifteen years. A rider who draws a high roller stands to win the most points. That's what makes those horses so valuable, the more they buck, the higher they fly, the more points a rider earns.'' Jake chuckled. ''That's if they can keep astride for the entire ride.''

''So you breed them?''

''Yep, most we do. But some aren't bred at all, some are just born that way. A rancher might call us up and say he's got a horse he can't break. John T. or Toby or me—we'll go check the horse out. If he looks like he's got potential, a horse inclined to buck, and we feel he'll make a good bucking horse, we'll take him on.''

Cassie watched the horses, listened to Jake's explanation, the excitement in his voice filling her senses. He had a look on his face that spoke of respect and appreciation, a regard for this special kind of ranching and the animals that struck a deep cord in her.

''A good bucking horse is worth a small fortune to a rodeo. It's what constitutes most of the wealth here. That and the pickup horses we raise.''

When Cassie appeared puzzled, Jake continued, ''Those are the horses that help out a rider when he's through with his ride. They have to be specially trained, both horse and rider being able to get close enough to the bronc buster to help him off the bucking horse. Most of the horses you see down at the corrals are pickup horses. We've got three mares ready to foal down there, too.''

Jake and Cassie stood silent for a moment, watching the untamed horses prance around, some nuzzled others, causing a quick short-lived fury and others simply grazed contentedly.

''How often do you come up here?'' Cassie asked, her

mind reeling. She hadn't a clue that Jake cared anything about the ranch. He'd never let on before, but now she was seeing a different side of him, perhaps a side he was finally willing to share with her.

"Whenever I'm in town, I help Toby with them."

"They're beautiful horses."

"Hmm. And they have a spirit that can't be held down. They'll go to their graves with that wildness still in them. They don't have to answer to anyone. Some of them work a total of ten minutes a year. That's all. The rest of the time they're free." Jake spoke with pride, his gaze resting on the animals.

"You really love it here, don't you?" Cassie saw it clearly now. Jake loved the land. He loved the ranch. He loved working with the stock. He couldn't disguise the passion in his voice and the brilliant gleam in his eyes. He might hide behind his words, he might run away to the rodeo, but there was no mistaking Jake's true calling. He was a rancher, whether he knew it or not.

Jake shrugged. "I like working with the stock."

Cassie smiled sadly. He liked working with the horses because he could relate to them. Their very nature, their untamed spirit and the way they answered to no one, called to Jake. He was just as they were, a soul that couldn't be held down, a spirit that had to be free.

Cassie sighed, understanding Jake better now. Nothing was going to hold this man down. Not the ranch, the baby, or a wife. Jake's idea to bring Cassie up here, might just have backfired, because Cassie knew without a doubt she could never marry Jake Griffin.

They drove back in silence with Cassie deep in thought, the idea of leaving the ranch nagging at her. She glanced sideways at Jake behind the wheel, wondering if she had the strength to leave him, to pack up all of her belongings and abandon the home she'd come to love.

Brian needed her. She would have family in Los Angeles, and the support of friends. Whenever Cassie thought long and hard about leaving, tears welled up in her eyes and she would put the notion out of her head, but soon she knew she'd have to make a decision.

As the truck pulled up to the main house, Marie came racing down the steps as fast as the elderly woman's legs could take her. With an ashen face and watery eyes, she cried, "Jake! Jake! Your father's had a heart attack. They took him to the hospital. You must go quick. Carson Memorial."

Jake bounded out of the truck. Cassie was just steps behind. "Are you okay, Marie?" Jake asked.

"I'm fine, I'm fine."

"Tell me what happened?"

Marie began to tremble. Jake wrapped his arm around her shoulder. "I found him in his study. He was slumped in the chair, having trouble breathing. He said it would pass, but I stayed with him and it didn't pass. When he clutched his chest, I begged him to let me call for help. The ambulance came and took him away. You must go to him."

"I will. But you have to promise me to go inside and calm down. I'll call you as soon as I know anything. Okay?"

"Okay," she said, relaxing a bit.

"Promise me, Marie?"

She nodded and Jake kissed her cheek, waiting until she climbed the steps of the main house. Jake huffed out a deep breath and turned to Cassie. "I'd better go."

"Not without me." She took his arm with reassuring pressure. "I'm going with you."

Jake nodded and they climbed back into the truck.

Eleven

"**I**'m fine, really. Just got to eat more vegetables," John T. stated, his pale face lighting up a bit when she and Jake entered his hospital room. They'd been kept waiting in the reception area for two hours while the doctors conducted a battery of tests on John T. Cassie had paced the floor, asking questions of the nurse, while Jake flipped through magazines. She knew he'd been concerned, but Jake Griffin, an expert at concealing his feelings, hadn't said much of anything. "I wish they'd hurry up and get these dang gadgets off me. I'm not a man comfortable with being hog-tied."

"Be patient, John T.," Lottie said, lovingly fingering wayward locks of his salt-and-pepper hair back into place. She'd been the first to arrive, never leaving John T.'s side. "The doctor says to take it easy."

Cassie walked over and bent down to give him a quick hug, making sure not to push aside any of the tubes hooked up to him. She kissed his cheek and smiled. "You gave us all a scare."

She backed up and stared at Jake, who as yet hadn't said a word. Jake blinked and stepped forward, putting out his hand. John T. immediately clasped it with both hands in what was more than a handshake. "The doc says you're going to be just fine."

"Thanks, son. A wake-up call is how the doc put it. He says I've got to cut out the greasy foods, exercise…"

"Not stress yourself out," Lottie added firmly. "And be doggone sure to take your medicine."

John T. glanced at Lottie; the loving look he shot her made Cassie smile. "You promised to see to that."

Lottie's tawny gaze stayed on him. "I always keep my promises."

They stared into each other's eyes for a long moment and Cassie thought the two needed privacy. She glanced at Jake, who had an unreadable expression on his face. "Maybe we should let John T. rest."

Lottie agreed. "Yes, the nurse said not to tire him out."

"I'm not a bit tired," he said, but pallid skin and sleepy eyes belied his adamant denial.

"But you will rest now, won't you?" Lottie asked, her sweet face filled with concern.

"Bossy woman. Yes, I'll rest, but after I speak with Cassie. It'll only take a minute or two."

Lottie nodded, glancing at Jake. "Come on, Jake," she said with a wink, "we know when we're not welcome. Let's grab us some coffee."

Cassie watched Lottie take Jake's arm and walk out of the room, then she turned to John T. His face paled considerably and he closed his eyes. Apparently, John T. was also good at hiding things, the heart attack, mild as it may have been, was certainly taking a toll on his body. "John T? Maybe I should let you rest. We can talk later."

He opened his eyes, shaking his head. "No, please. I won't rest until I say my piece. Have a seat, Cassie."

Cassie slid a chair close to John T.'s right side and waited. Sterile hospital sounds surrounded her, the loudspeaker overhead signaling doctors and the quiet hustle of nurses at work, jolted her into reality. The idea of John T., such a vital, strong man diminished by illness, greatly upset her.

John T. took a deep breath, his face somber and his sharp eyes filled with concern. "A lot goes through a man's mind when he's being carted off to the hospital. Your life sort of flashes by, all the mistakes, all the things you wished you'd done differently, but mostly, you think about the people in your life. The ones who are most important to you."

"Are you talking about Jake?"

He nodded slowly. "Jake, well, he hasn't come around as I'd hoped. He's a good man. I know that in my heart, but he's been hurt bad, and it's my fault.... I'm fearful for my son. He's been a loner all his life. He's never let anyone in and he's never seemed to need anyone. Until now. I think my son needs you, Cassie. Even though he's too pigheaded to admit it, he cares for you deeply. I see the way he looks at you. I've caught sight of the two of you together on the ranch and there's something powerful there. I'll tell you, until you came here to the ranch, I'd just about lost all hope with him, but now, well, I think you're his best chance for a happy life."

Cassie shook her head. Just hours ago, up at the north pasture, she'd pretty much discounted any real future with Jake. "I don't know, John T."

"Lottie sort of hinted that you're not too happy here anymore. I'm real sorry about that. I know it has to do with

Jake and the way he's been treating you. I'm just asking you to give him a chance. Don't make any hasty decisions. No sense pretending I don't want my grandchild being born on the ranch, but it's more than that, Cassie. I'm asking you, for Jake. Stay and try to work things out.''

Cassie doubted John T. pleaded with anyone about anything, and to see him so open, so vulnerable and honest, tugged at her heart. She couldn't leave the ranch now, more so than ever, until she was certain John T. would recover fully. She couldn't abandon him in the face of the friendship they'd developed. She took hold of his hand, being careful not to nudge the IV out of place on his arm, and squeezed gently. ''Of course I'll stay, John T. The decisions I have to make can wait until you're fully recovered.''

''Thank you, Cassie. It's all I ask.''

''Maybe I should let you rest. Lottie will have my hide if I stay too long.''

John T. grinned. ''She's a dynamo, that one, isn't she?''

''She cares about you.''

''Yeah, I doubt that I deserve her. She clamored in here the minute she arrived, claiming to be my wife. She actually told those nurses we were married so she could see me. When I saw her, with her heart in her eyes, I figured I'd been a fool long enough. Then I figured, why not? I don't know how many more years I have left, no sense wasting them. I've loved that woman for many years, just was too damn scared to do anything about it.''

Pleasantly stunned, Cassie asked, ''What were you afraid of?''

He reached for Cassie's hand, and she was amazed at the strength he exhibited, the press of his hand upon hers. With eyes softer than she'd ever seen them, he spoke with regret. ''I'd made a mess of every relationship I've ever been in. Didn't want to chance losing Lottie's friendship. But, it seemed I almost lost her, anyway, with my mule-headed ways. So I up and asked her to marry me this afternoon. Wasn't going to say anything to anybody until I got out of the hospital, but knowing Lottie she's probably spilling the beans to Jake as we speak.''

Cassie had to physically contain her joy. She wanted to leap up from her chair, but knew she couldn't disrupt John T. and the hold he had on her hand. ''You asked her to marry you! That's wonderful, John T. I couldn't be happier. What did Lottie say?''

John T.'s face wrinkled, as if puzzled by Lottie's reaction, but a soft, quizzical smile emerged, anyway. ''It was the darnedest thing. I'm pretty sure she meant yes, but she said, 'Hot molasses!' ''

John T. was grumpier than an old polecat trapped in a wire cage, Lottie had stated plainly, and she'd let the man know from the get-go that she wouldn't put up with his tirades. Cassie had to admit Lottie had a soothing effect on him, keeping the man calm and settling him into a routine he'd rather not adhere to. But with or without his cooperation, Lottie Fairchild would see to his recovery. Cassie was grateful that she'd come by every day since he'd been released from the hospital one week ago. Her presence at the ranch allowed both she and Jake to take over the ranch duties. As they handled their new responsibilities she and Jake began to realize just how much John T. had done to keep his empire strong and prosperous.

At times Jake had seemed restless, too, almost seeming trapped, or afraid that if John T. took a turn for the worse, he'd be next in line to run the ranch. He was the heir to Anderson Ranch, whether he liked that fact or not. It was a constant puzzle to Cassie, knowing how much he loved the ranch, yet she saw indecision in his eyes, fear perhaps, too, whenever she found him lost in thought. Jake fought his true place here at Anderson Ranch with a tireless vengeance, it seemed, and if his father's heart attack couldn't break down his defenses, Cassie believed, nothing would.

Cassie logged off the computer in her office and took a moment for herself. She stood up and stretched her arms overhead, yawning once, then again, realizing she'd been up before dawn, diligent at work. The knock at her door was welcomed. She fluffed her hair and straightened out her shirt, tucking it into her now-tight jeans. Soon she'd have to think about making a trip to the maternity store.

"Hey, Lottie. Taking a break?" She let her friend in.

"That, and Jake sent over these requisitions for you. He said there's no rush. Whenever you have time to look them over is fine." She walked over to the kitchen table and plopped the forms down, then turned to give Cassie a big smile. "He also said to keep tonight open."

Cassie blinked. Since John T.'s heart attack, they hadn't had much time together, alone or otherwise, other than the business they conducted for Anderson Ranch. "Did he say why?"

Lottie chuckled, a deep throaty sound. "If I had to guess, I'd say it had nothing to do with business. Well, maybe... monkey business." Lottie let go a full-fledged laugh this time, her delight so contagious, Cassie joined in.

"Oh, I don't know what I'm going to do with that man," Cassie admitted once their laughter died down.

Lottie kept the smile in her eyes. "Give him a chance, honey."

That's what John T. had asked. "Don't you think I have been?"

Lottie kept her gaze steady and the directness of her answer startled Cassie. "You've been busy protecting your heart. Now, I can understand that, but maybe if you surrender it, just a little, Jake will come to trust you. I know it's a hard thing, putting yourself out there, hoping not to get crushed, but Jake might need that from you. He's never had anyone put his or her heart on the line for him before. Do you get what I'm saying?''

Cassie had never thought of it that way before. She had been busy protecting herself. But that was a natural reaction for a woman who'd been burned before. She was the classic example of gun-shy. She'd fought her feelings for Jake, pushing him aside, rejecting him at every turn. But Lottie might be right. Jake might need a woman who would surrender the fight. Maybe he was unknowingly looking for someone ready to take everything he could dish out and still come out unscathed and wanting him, earning his loyalty, trust and maybe even his love.

Cassie didn't know if she could be that woman.

She didn't know if she wouldn't crumble under his fire. She didn't know if given a chance, Jake wouldn't permanently break her fragile heart.

She didn't just want to be married to the father of her child. She wanted to be loved by a man who couldn't live without her. There was a giant-size difference, even if Jake couldn't or wouldn't, see that.

Her reply came out in a breathy whisper. ''I get what you're saying, Lottie.''

Lottie hugged Cassie, apparently aware she'd sobered up the moment. ''Come on, girl. We both deserve a little break. John T. has promised to take an afternoon nap, so we can go into town and do us a little shopping. I've got a purse full of money and I want to buy the baby something nice. There's this brand-new baby store you have to see.''

That evening Cassie sat across from Jake in an elegant restaurant on the north shore of Lake Tahoe, the majestic view of the emerald water a remarkable sight to behold. He'd taken her on an hour-long scenic drive along the lake just as the sun descended the horizon, claiming a need for both of them to relax after the grueling week they'd spent overseeing the ranch and worrying over John T.

When he'd appeared on her doorstep, dressed in a black Western suit, bolo tie, wearing that darn sexy black Stetson, Cassie didn't have the heart to decline his invitation, spit-shiny black boots and all. He'd given her carte blanche, all the time she needed to get ready, happy to sit in the living room and wait. Cassie had never dressed so fast in her life. A woman had to be far too sure of herself to keep such a tempting man waiting for long. Cassie didn't have that much confidence. Yet her efforts had paid off. Jake's gaze had followed her into the room, watching her every move with a prideful gleam of appreciation.

He lifted his glass of sparkling cider in a toast. Cassie had been pleased at his consideration, although she'd assured him she wouldn't mind his drinking something that packed a punch. Jake declined any alcoholic beverage. ''To you, Cassie. I'm a lucky man to have such a beautiful woman as my date.''

Cassie touched her own glass of cider to his. ''Thank you, Jake. This is a treat. I didn't realize how worn out I was this week. And just in time, too. I don't know how much longer I'll be fitting into my dress clothes.'' With a maternal hand she laid her palm on her stomach, wondering about his comment. Was she really his date? Was he trying to court her? Heavens, she was carrying his child and they had come so far, but they'd never really dated.

Jake took a slow, leisurely tour of her body, his gaze traveling along at snail-like pace, touching each part of her, his dark, studious eyes meeting hers, then moving along to her mouth, tempting her with a hot, hungry look and then lower yet, to linger on her breasts, enough to make her nipples peak with urgent awareness. It was a good thing he couldn't see any farther down, where her legs pressed together, tightening with need and desire.

Cassie fanned her face, shaking her wrist, the wave of her fingers thwarting the flame of the candlelight. "Whew, sure is warm in here."

Jake loosened his tie and took off his jacket, a move that made Cassie heat up even more. "I know what you mean," he said, a seductive gleam lighting his eyes. "You look gorgeous in green, makes your eyes look as vivid as the water in Emerald Bay, but I was sort of hoping you'd wear the black dress."

The one she'd worn the night they'd made love.

"It holds one magic memory for me."

Pregnant with his child, Cassie didn't think he could do or say anything that would bring a blush to her face. But then, Jake Griffin always surprised her.

Cassie gulped down her drink, trying not to choke on the amber liquid, trying to keep her head and her heart intact. Little did he know, Cassie had almost worn that dress tonight, but decided she'd be better off retiring the garment to Cassie Munroe's Hall of Fame. That dress held magic memories for her, as well.

A short time later Cassie stood on the porch to the guest house, Jake beside her, as he'd been most of the night. They'd had a quiet drive home, Cassie taking sideway glances at him every chance she could. The man had discarded his jacket for the drive, taken off his tie and undone the top three buttons on his shirt. All Cassie could think about was slipping her hand in there, running her fingers through the soft curls of his chest and grazing her palm along his hot, muscled skin.

She turned the key in the lock.

''Invite me in, Cassie,'' he said softly, his seductive words as enticing as the sultry night air. He stood behind her, his scent enveloping her, a mixture of manly soap and spicy aftershave. ''For coffee.'' He kissed her throat.

''Sorry, fresh out of coffee.'' She spoke automatically, the lie slipping from her lips as her body trembled uncontrollably.

''For soda.'' He kissed her again, this time nibbling her neck as if she were a delectable dessert. His body full up against her, Cassie knew they'd bypass the kitchen entirely, barely hoping to make it to the bedroom.

''D-don't h-have any of that e-either.''

Jake turned her into his arms, a smile lifting the corners of his mouth. ''For water, then. You wouldn't deny a thirsty man, would you?'' he asked softly, running a finger down her throat. He played with the soft swell of her breast, gliding his fingers just under the edge of her bodice, meeting with the lace of her bra and farther, creating tingles and an ache Cassie felt deep, deep inside. Her skin prickled from his bold caress and a sharp pang of desire put her entire body on alert.

''That…might not be a good idea,'' she murmured.

''Can't think of a better one, darlin','' he claimed, then he bent his head and sipped from her lips, a tender brush of his mouth that left her wanting. Wanting. ''I'm gonna miss you when I'm gone.''

''Gone?'' Cassie came out of the seductive haze Jake had so expertly engulfed her in. ''Are you leaving again?''

''Tomorrow. First thing.''

''But John T.'s only been out of the hospital for a week.''

Jake smiled. ''He's a tough codger, Cassie. And Lottie won't leave his side. I've cleared off all the work until Monday. I have to go. But I'm not going far, just up to Reno.

Won't take but little more than an hour to make it back home if I'm needed.''

Cassie closed her eyes and nodded. He'd only be gone three days, but she'd gotten accustomed to having Jake around this week. She knew she'd miss him terribly. "Have a good trip," was all she could think to say.

He kissed her lightly and backed away. She watched him descend the porch steps, but before reaching his truck he stopped and pivoted on his boot heels. "Ah, hell." Climbing back up the steps in long, quick, purposeful strides, he faced her within seconds and she was in his arms again, his kiss this time not tender, not gentle, but a mad, crazy crushing of their mouths, his body pressing hot and hard against hers. He gave her no time to think, no time to breathe.

His mouth took claim, holding nothing back, and the extent of his desire, the dire need, completely evident with the rub of his granite body on hers. He drove his tongue deep into her mouth, probing, searching and then conquering until Cassie went weak in the knees. Her legs barely held her. Luckily she had the door to her back, her only support other than the man who had her pressed solidly against him. Between the two, Cassie thought, she might just keep upright.

"Come with me, Cassie." He broke the kiss, breathing heavily. "Come with me," he urged.

No was her first instinct. She couldn't go. It was a dangerous thought. And what about John T. and her work? No. No. She couldn't. But a compelling voice echoed in her head.

Give him a chance.
Surrender, just a little.
Put it all on the line for him.

Lottie's words, her advice, jolted her senses. She stared deep into Jake's searching dark eyes and saw the raw need there, the hope mingled with desire. And Cassie knew she couldn't reject him. She couldn't deny him. She didn't have the willpower or the inclination to deprive them both the opportunity for happiness. She'd gotten all of her work caught up. And Jake was right about Lottie. She wouldn't leave John T.'s side. Besides, isn't this exactly what John T. had asked of her, also? He'd be the first one to tell her to go.

Cassie would go. She'd put her heart out there, hoping Jake wouldn't trample it. She'd muster her courage and let go her protective instincts. If she were to be a fool, she'd be a happy one. "Yes, yes, Jake. I'll go with you." *I'll take the chance.*

"You mean it?" His smile was as wide as a schoolboy who'd won first prize in a spelling bee. Was Cassie his prize? Apparently at the moment. He lifted her gently and swirled her around in his arms. Her feet hit the ground with a soft thud.

But Cassie was certain she was still floating on air.

The next morning Cassie sat in Jake's truck as they drove north to Reno, his horse trailer hitched in the back, carting Shadow and Jake's other rodeo horse, a sleek roan named Strawberry Wine. "On long drives I have to stop every four or five hours to water the horses, but today's drive is easy. I'll have them corralled up at the rodeo grounds in no time. Then I have a surprise for you."

Cassie turned to gaze into Jake's smug face. She narrowed her eyes, and gave him a tilt of her head, wondering what kind of surprise Jake had in mind for her. "I don't like surprises," she teased.

A killer smile flashed Jake's sparkling teeth and lit his brown eyes with amusement. "You're gonna like this one."

A short time later, after Jake had signed in at the rodeo grounds and taken care of his horses, true to his word, he'd surprised her. They pulled up to the house Cassie had lived in as a young girl in the small rural town of Tyler, just twenty minutes outside of Reno. "Jake! How did you know?"

Cassie sat dumbfounded in the truck, gazing out at the small cottage-like home she and Brian had been raised in as children with their folks. Jake bounded out of the truck and before she knew it, he had opened her door and helped her down. "I called Brian."

Cassie stood on the elm-lined street, gazing into his eyes with stunned surprise. "My brother, Brian? You spoke with him?"

"Yep. And after I got my ear chewed off for about ten minutes, he finally gave me the address."

Cassie was too thrilled about Jake's surprise to ask him what Brian had said to him. She shuddered inwardly, figuring it was best not to know. She knew Brian and his temper could stand up to Jake's on any day of the week. "This is a wonderful surprise, thank you," she said softly, turning to glance once again at the home that had meant so much to her. She'd had great memories of her young life here, when both of her parents had been alive. They'd been a family for too short a time. "It's yellow now, but the shutters are still white. When I lived here, the house was peacock-blue." She chuckled. Her mother loved blue. Everything inside the home was some shade of blue, the kitchen, sky-blue, the living room, a baby blue, and Cassie's room, a blue-green that one would define as turquoise but her mother had insisted on calling shallow-waters blue.

A young woman hustled out of the home next door, chasing a small child, catching their attention. "Brendan James, you come back here right now." The woman caught the laughing boy in her arms, her voice not demanding but playful. "I've got you now!"

She stopped up short when she spotted Cassie, her gaze making a quick sweep of her face. "Oh, my God! Cassandra, is that you?"

Cassie stepped forward tentatively. "Cynthia? Cynthia Graham. Oh, my goodness!" Cassie approached her childhood friend with a big smile. Years washed away as Cassie noted that Cynthia looked exactly the same, with light brown hair and scattered freckles on her wholesome face. "I can't believe it's you! Do you still live here?"

"Yes, yes I do. My parents retired and moved south to San Juan Capistrano. They gave us the house as a wedding present."

"You're married and this darling boy must be your son?" Cassie smiled at the blond-headed boy. "Hello."

The child hugged his mother's neck, suddenly shy. "Say hello, Brendan. This is my friend, Cassandra."

"You can call me Cassie," she said to both mother and son. Brendan only smiled slightly. "And this is my friend, Jake Griffin." Cassie turned to find Jake leaning casually against the cab of his truck, arms crossed, wearing a big grin, but his gaze, his sole focus, rested on the little boy. Deep yearning gleamed from his dark eyes as he studied adorable Brendan James. Cassie's throat constricted and her heart leaped forcefully in her chest.

Jake moved away from the truck, putting a hand out to Cynthia. "Nice to meet you." They shook hands briefly. "Hello, buddy," he said to Brendan.

The little boy stared up at Jake. "Cowboy."

"Well, you could say that," Jake said, and then the boy reached up to touch the brim of Jake's hat.

"Hat." The boy's eyes gleamed with interest.

"That's right, it's a h-a-t," Cynthia said in a motherly tone that Cassie knew she'd come to use, also, one day soon.

"My goodness, this is quite a nice surprise. Do you have time for a drink so we can catch up?"

Cassie glanced at Jake and he nodded. "I don't have to be at the rodeo until later in the afternoon."

Half an hour later Cassie sat with Cynthia on the back porch, sipping her second glass of lemonade. She figured they'd bored the boys with all the "catching up" they'd done, so when Jake offered to play a game with Brendan James, the boy was only too eager to agree. They watched as Jake tossed a big rubber ball to Brendan on the backyard lawn. "He's a good catch for a two-year-old," Cassie said, admiring the child.

"He loves to play. His father plays ball with him whenever he can. Chuck is a firefighter so his shifts vary from week to week. Brendan loves it when Daddy is home. But he's usually shy with strangers. Jake is good with children, I see. Brendan took to him immediately."

Cassie swallowed hard, the ache at seeing Jake so patient and caring with Brendan, twisting a knot in her stomach. She knew Jake would make a great father. Was she so wrong to deny him that chance on a permanent basis?

Perhaps, this weekend alone with Jake would change things. Maybe, once Cassie bared her heart and soul to him, he'd let go his bitterness and mistrust. Cassie was willing to put it all on the line for Jake. Glancing again at Brendan's joyous face and Jake giving gentle instruction to the boy, Cassie knew she had to try. "Yes," Cassie said to Cynthia softly, seeing firsthand what she'd always presumed. "Jake is very good with children."

Twelve

Cassie took one last glance at herself in the hotel mirror, unnecessarily adjusting the black satin dress that fit her perfectly, the one she'd worn the night she and Jake had created their baby. She ran shaky fingers through her hair and puckered her lips, making sure the lip-gloss was applied evenly. Jake would be here any second. After his rodeo event they'd had a wonderful dinner at the Silverado Hotel's finest restaurant. And after, he'd had to make a personal appearance at the rodeo carnival where he would meet fans and sign autographs, but Cassie had begged off, claiming slight fatigue.

Jake had hesitated at first, his indecision evident as to whether to leave her alone or not, but Cassie had insisted she needed to rest and that she'd be fine. In truth, she'd planned a surprise for him.

Something she hoped he would appreciate.

When she heard the front door opening, she sucked in a

breath. Here she was, laying her heart on the line for him and secretly praying she wasn't making another "Classic Cassie" mistake.

Candles lit the room in quiet elegance. Champagne chilled in a bucket, and a small chocolate cake burning a single thin white candle sat atop the marble tabletop. Cassie met him in the middle of the suite, her smile wide, her heart pounding. "Happy Birthday, Jake."

Jake stopped dead in his tracks, his face masking emotion as his gaze darted around the room. Finally he focused his attention on her. Cassie held her breath. In his dress Western gear—new jeans, crisp, black-studded shirt and shiny polished silver buckle—Jake looked irresistible. "How did you know?"

"It's just past midnight and officially your birthday. A little bird told me," she teased. Bravely she walked over to him. "I thought we could have a little private celebration."

Jake slammed his eyes shut, saying nothing, but his body trembled and the slide of his Adam's apple in a big swallow, told her all she needed to know. Cassie took his hand and led him over to the sofa where she made him sit down. She lowered herself next to him. Softly she added, "There's chocolate cake, champagne for you, juice for me, a candle for you to wish upon and more."

His eyes met hers. "More?"

She nodded. "Much more." She kissed him tenderly on the lips. It was all the invitation he needed. He kissed her back with heat, a passion that seemed to explode into hot fragments of desire. His hands went into her hair, threading through as he leaned her back, kissing her chin, her throat, the sensitive swell of her breasts. She tingled immediately from Jake's touch. Shooting sparks traveled a speedy trail to all of her female parts, her nipples especially sensitive. Carrying a child had some great advantages. Every erotic sensation thrilled her to heightened peaks. But she knew that would only be true with Jake. No other man compared to him in that regard.

"This is the best birthday celebration I've ever had, darlin'."

"I was hoping you'd like it."

"You wore the dress," he said in a soft tone that belied the fire in his eyes.

"This old thing?" she teased, plucking at the material as if it were nothing more than a dishrag.

"Old thing?" He chuckled, then a wickedly sinful light gleamed in his eyes. "You're right. Looks like it's just about ready to fall apart. Might as well take it off you."

He turned her around and began the seductive slow release of the garment, kissing each inch of the skin he bared. Tingles shot straight through her, creating fiery heat inside, but Cassie couldn't give in to her desire just yet. She wanted to do this right. She wanted Jake to celebrate, to know that his birthday was important, that *he* was important and that it meant something to her. "We'll have cake, Jake, and a drink to begin with," she said, glancing at him over her shoulder.

Jake undid the dress entirely and she turned to witness deep appreciation in his eyes as he raked over her near naked body. She wore black lacy underwear. He groaned and repeated her words with regret. "We'll have cake and a drink."

She smiled. And he pulled her into his lap. "That's better," he said, nuzzling her hair, breathing in her scent and stroking the skin just above her breasts. One finger played provocatively with the delicate lace on her bra. Her skin prickled from his heady ministrations and the area between her thighs began to throb. "You wouldn't want me to have a heart attack on my birthday."

She might be the one to have the heart attack. If Jake didn't quit caressing her that way, no telling what sort of irregular jolts her heart might have. "No, just cake and—"

"You?"

"That's right, cowboy. And me."

He was rock-hard underneath her. "Hurry up and cut the cake, Cassie."

"Make a wish, Jake. And blow out your candle."

Jake grinned. "I'm getting my wish tonight." He blew out the candle.

Cassie cut the cake with a small knife. She brought it up to his mouth and fed it to him, deliberately smearing the frosting on his face. She ran her tongue along his chin, his cheek, licking off the mess she'd made. He groaned, as if in terrible pain, but remained where she had him, pretty much at her mercy. She applied light pressure to his mouth, her tongue stroking over, giving him a taste of cake and a taste of her.

"Do you like the taste?" she asked, licking at his mouth once more.

An anguished sound escaped his throat, telling Cassie she'd probably gone too far. Jake grabbed her tight and lowered her down on the sofa. He stared deep into her eyes; his, incredibly dark and hungry. "Forget the champagne, darlin'. I appreciate the thought, but you've got me ready to combust."

With one quick move the snaps of his shirt came apart and he flung it, without care, exposing his chest, the burn of his skin meeting with hers. Cassie thrilled at his strength, the stunning supple muscles of his flaming body. He was firm where she was soft and the contrast, the press of his skin on hers, made her dizzy with passion.

His lips were back on hers immediately, the tang of his spicy aftershave mingling with chocolate cake and the scent of the candle, a sexy combination of aromas that heightened Cassie's awareness even more.

"I can't wait any longer," he murmured. "I've waited too long for you." She heard the slide of his zipper and within a moment they were one, Jake taking her with single elemental purpose. His body joined with hers, a perfect union that bordered on ecstasy. Cassie released a small moan of pleasure and waited. Perfectly still, Jake looked down into her eyes. "The baby?"

Cassie assured the concerned father-to-be, "Is fine, Jake. Making love won't hurt him."

With relief evident on his face, Jake bent his head to kiss her. Through the filmy haze of desire, Cassie realized her sexy cowboy had failed to remove his jeans and boots. The erotic thought seeped into her soul, bringing thrilling shivers of excitement as Jake continued his tender assault. He left no part of her body untouched and with urgent caresses and expert finesse he brought them both to a quick and satisfying release.

She breathed out his name, and he, hers. They lay joined for a moment more, to catch their breaths, then Jake stood, took her into his arms, making a sweep for the champagne bottle as he carried her into the bedroom. "Now that we've gotten the first go round out of the way, it's time for the finals."

Cassie stared into his eyes, a smile playing on her lips. "I love it when you talk rodeo, cowboy."

Every bone in her body ached for Jake again. She needed him as she needed oxygen in her lungs. She relished being with him, being in his arms and the way he had of making her feel cherished and beautiful.

Gently, he set her down on the bed then flung off his boots and stripped out of his jeans. Cassie watched in awe as the man with sleek moves and dangerous grace came down beside her. His breathtaking muscular form astounded her. He was all man, a rugged, sexy cowboy. And for tonight, he was all hers.

He took her into his arms. "Sweetheart, I've got enough rodeo talk to keep you happy for a lifetime."

Cassie ignored his gentle hint to turn the tables, using a bit of rodeo talk to tease him. "Are you a high roller, Jake?"

Jake burst out laughing, his eyes warm with invitation at the reminder of the herd of high-flying bucking horses they'd viewed at the ranch. His eyebrows rose up provocatively as he lifted her to straddle his thighs. He set her down slowly, carefully, impaling her with his rigid manhood.

He responded with a slow, sexy drawl, "Darlin', it'll be my pleasure to show you."

Morning dawned and Jake woke up next to a thoroughly rumpled Cassie. Satisfaction, a contented sensation he'd never experienced before, settled in his gut. He rolled over and gently laid his arm across her, possessively, trying not to wake her, but the need to hold her, to keep her by his side, was too strong to fight.

She was a unique woman, he admitted, unlike any other he'd ever met. She was soft now, unguarded, appearing peaceful as she took quiet breaths. But when the woman was awake she was as spirited as the mares they raised at the ranch, and he liked that about her. She'd continually shocked and surprised him time and again, not always pleasantly. Her refusal to marry him rankled. He'd offered her all that he had, all that he could, yet she still had refused.

But her sweet birthday surprise had hit him straight in the heart. She'd done for him, what no other ever had. She'd made the day special, and even if they hadn't had mind-blowing sex last night, Jake still would never forget the softness in her eyes, her eagerness to please him and to celebrate the day of his birth. He hadn't ever had a reason to celebrate before this, but being with her changed all that. She'd given him a reason. She and the baby were the reason.

But they had had incredible sex. And as Jake peered down at her, those expressive green eyes, still calmly closed, the spiky ginger hair and that sassy mouth of hers stirred him again.

Hell, he wanted her.

Jake figured they could make love all day, right here in this room, and he'd never tire of her. It wasn't a bad plan since the calf roping finals weren't until tomorrow. Except by then he'd be so worn out he probably wouldn't have the strength to toss the damn rope.

He let go a long sigh and rolled away from her.

Confusing thoughts crowded his head. He struggled with warring emotions. All of his adult life he'd set out to win the rodeo championship, to prove a point, to make John T. stand up and take notice that Jake didn't need him or the ranch. He was his own man. When he'd needed his father—really needed him while growing up—the man was too busy with his *real* family and building his empire to give him a thought.

Now the rodeo was all Jake had. And the baby. His baby. A child he wouldn't abandon. No matter what Cassie had to say about it, Jake Griffin was going to raise his own child. He had months to make her change her mind.

He glanced at her once more, a quiet groan erupting in his throat watching the sunlight stream onto her body, only half sheathed with a sheet. He tossed his sheet aside and climbed out of bed.

The woman needed her rest.

And Jake needed a cold shower.

* * *

Water sounds woke her. Cassie opened her eyes to find Jake gone from their bed. She rose slowly and followed the sound until she stood outside the frosted-glass shower door in the bathroom.

She debated half a second, then opened the door and joined him, all the while repeating the mantra in her head. *Lay it all on the line for him.*

"Hi." Hot steam assailed her first, then water rained down in a warm rush that soothed as it cleansed.

Jake grinned. "I was just thinking about you."

She wrapped her arms around his neck and on tiptoes, kissed his cheek, the shower spray hitting them both in the face. "Anything good?"

He took her in his arms, bringing his back up against the intricately tiled shower wall. "Everything good."

He brought her close, his body pressing against hers, sleek, and hard and wet. Cassie sighed. His voice took on a sultry tone. "You ever make love in a shower before?" A tick worked at his jaw then and a frown stole over his face. "Never mind. I don't want to know."

"No. No, Jake. I've never experienced anything this... wonderful before." And Cassie meant it. Her lovemaking experience had been limited, and she knew Jake didn't want her explanation of details, just as she'd die knowing of the women who had come before her. But she had to in some small way let him know that he was the one man she wanted to experience new things with, the one man whom she'd surrender her heart to.

Jake bent his head, kissed her soundly on the lips and spoke softly. "Me, either."

Her heart soared with that bit of knowledge and all conversation drained away. Jake turned her around and Cassie thought she'd faint from what he had in mind, but then the fresh scent of apples assailed her. Jake poured a dollop of shampoo in her hair and Cassie relaxed and smiled as strong fingers lathered it in, massaging, caressing and scrubbing her hair squeaky clean.

''All clean,'' he said, tugging her hair gently, pulling her back against him. He wrapped his arms around her, stroking her torso, then farther up, until both hands cupped her breasts from behind. He played havoc with her then, caressing, teasing and rubbing her nipples until she wanted to die from the sensual torment.

Her wet skin met with his. Their bodies clung to each other. There was no mistaking Jake's arousal as it pressed into her in provocative places.

He kissed the back of her neck and spun her around. With a bar of almond scented soap in his hand, he began a slow, torturous seduction, moving the slippery soap over her skin. He started at her throat, making small circles, then moved the bar down to loop around one breast, bubbles lathering up. Jake blew them aside and put his mouth there, suckling and kissing, her nipples sensitive to his touch, peaking and aching for him. He did the same to the other side and when he left that responsive area, Cassie felt a keen sense of loss.

He cleaned her arms next, then bent to work on her legs, slipping the bar over her skin in a sensual assault, each inch he covered bringing her closer and closer to some unfathomable, erotic crest. Her skin prickled, her limbs ached, her body demanded even more.

Jake worked his way higher, moving up her thighs, gliding the soap over her legs. He stood up then, his manhood primed and ready, but he held back and used the soapy bar once again to caress her most sensitive spot. Cassie nearly bucked when he discarded the soap, working magic on her with expert fingers. She leaned into him and moaned, the moist wet pleasure, the stroking, almost too much. She gasped, "I need you, Jake."

"You have me, Cassie." Jake crushed his mouth to hers, driving his tongue deep at the exact moment he entered her. Intense heat shot straight through her. Water splashed, playing and surrounding them in a cloud of steam and moisture.

Jake groaned into her mouth, cupped her bottom and drove deeper, harder. She met each of his thrusts with one of her own. Cassie cried out, wrapping her legs around him, and they moved with each other until the impact nearly consumed them.

"Oh, Cassie."

Their release was powerful, spontaneous and timed to perfection.

Cassie relaxed against Jake, her body sated, her heart pouring out with love. He held her in his arms for long moments after turning the water off. She felt the exact moment when Jake's body let go the tension that was the aftermath of incredible lovemaking. His breathing slowed and he spoke softly into her ear. "We're good together, sweetheart."

Cassie closed her eyes and held back tears. Yes, they were great together, as long as Jake had everything in his control. As long as Cassie was giving up her heart to him, but those were not the three words she'd wanted to hear.

She stepped out of the shower and toweled off, determined not to think of this as a setback. They still had time together. She had to wear down Jake's defenses, make him see he could trust her with his heart. But there was one more thing she had failed to do. She promised herself she'd try again. She wouldn't give up.

Jake had called room service and shortly after their shower, breakfast was delivered. Cassie stood over the table by the hotel window, peering down at the trays of food "Are you expecting rodeo riders in here, or maybe we're going to feed Shadow and Strawberry Wine with all this food?"

"Nah, the horses don't like waffles," he said with a wink, "but I'm starved. Sort of worked up an appetite last night."

Heat warmed her face, but she chuckled along with him. "Jake."

He came to stand behind her and laid a hand on her abdomen, caressing the skin from under her blouse. "Our baby has to eat. And so does his mama." He kissed the area just below her earlobe, sending shivers along her spine. After the night and morning they'd just shared, Cassie didn't think she'd have enough energy to become aroused again, but then, this was Jake, the man she loved, the man who could, with just one look, turn her inside out. "Do you think it's a boy or a girl?"

He continued to caress her belly, the heat of his hand flooding her entire body with warmth. She hesitated. Every time they got on the subject of the baby, they argued. Cassie hadn't changed her mind, although many times during the night, while she was in Jake's arms, the temptation to give in and give up crossed her mind. How easy it would be to agree to marry him, to be his wife, but then what—live life devoid of love? To know the lust of each other's body but share nothing else in return?

Cassie gave herself a mental head shake. Nope. She wasn't going to go that route, no matter how much she loved Jake or how hard it was to deny his marriage proposals. "I haven't a clue. Sometime later on I can find out, but I'm not so sure I want to know. Boy or girl, I want to be surprised."

"I want to be there, Cassie. When our baby is born."

"I—I know. I want you there."

"And I want us to be married by then."

Cassie stepped away from him, away from the press of his body, the warmth of his hand on her skin. She needed to regroup, to firm up her resolve. "Jake, let's not talk about that right now."

Anger flashed across his face, a wildfire of emotion so deep and intense, Cassie thought to run from the room. He glared at her, then spoke through tight lips. "You won't even think about it?"

"I am thinking about it."

His face registered a degree of relief, a remotely surprised expression as if to say he had doubted that she'd even consider the idea. Cassie wanted to scream from frustration. She didn't want to hurt Jake. She didn't want to deny him his baby. This weekend she had hoped to show Jake that he could trust her and to get him to open up his heart.

She spoke softly but with an urgency that stemmed from the ache in her heart. "Please, don't rush me. And please, don't bully me, either. That's not what'll make me change my mind."

"What will, then, Cassie? How can I change your mind?"

Cassie bit down on her lower lip and moved across the room to the telephone. "Your father's been ill, Jake. We've been gone for two days." She picked up the receiver and held it out to him. "Call him, Jake. See how John T. is doing."

Jake walked over to her, peering into her face. Then he stared at the telephone receiver she held. Long moments passed. Cassie witnessed the indecision on his face, the hard line of his jaw, the cold steel in his dark eyes. He took the receiver out of her hand and placed it back on its cradle.

''This is about you and me, Cassie. John T. has nothing to do with it.''

Oh, Jake, she wanted to scream. Your father has everything to do with it.

He went on, his gaze focused on the phone. ''Lottie's with him. She would have called if anything went wrong.''

''That's not really the point, now, is it?''

Jake spun around to stare her down. ''The point is, John T. Anderson hasn't been much of a father to me, Cassie.''

''Maybe that was true in the past, but he's trying, Jake. You can't say he hasn't tried.''

Jake shook his head. ''It's too late.''

''No,'' Cassie said, taking his hand. She led him over to the sofa to sit down, their meal all but forgotten. ''It's never too late for forgiveness. Do you plan on punishing him for the rest of your life?''

Jake twisted his mouth. ''It's easy for you to judge me, Cassie. You don't have the memories I have. Maybe you lost your parents at a young age, but you had an aunt that loved you and a brother who'd kick anybody's ass who did you wrong.''

Cassie chuckled. ''Did Brian say that to you?''

Jake squeezed her hand gently. ''In so many words. I have to say, I admire the guy. I couldn't even get ticked at him for sticking up for you. Even though you're the one holding out on the marriage, not me. But no one's ever been on my side like that before. I've never known that kind of loyalty.''

''It's love, Jake. My brother loves me. Just like John T. loves you. He does, you know. He made mistakes, there's no denying that, but he finally did the right thing. And he wants a chance to make it up to you.''

''You think if John Junior hadn't died, John T. would

have given me a second thought? Do you think he'd ever have come for me that night otherwise?''

Cassie ached for him, for the pain and regret she witnessed in his eyes. He tried to conceal it, tried to cover up the injury done to him, but Cassie knew him now, too well. His wounds went deep. ''I don't know, Jake. I really can't say.''

''It was the night of your homecoming, Cassie. That's why I didn't make our date. The father I never knew about showed up at the Brewsters's door with a social worker, claiming that I was his long-lost son. He whisked me away so quickly I never had time to adjust. I never had time to call the girl I liked to tell her I wasn't going to show for our date, to tell her I'd probably never see her again.''

''Oh, Jake.'' As a heartbroken teen Cassie had berated him over and over again in her mind, thinking that handsome, lone wolf, Jake Griffin, had found something lacking in her. Thinking that she had been conveniently duped then dumped. She'd been so wrapped up in her own anguish that she'd never once considered what Jake had gone through that night. She'd never contemplated the possibility that something devastating might have happened to him. No one had known too much about the boy who'd come to school midstream and had disappeared rather quickly, shortly after the homecoming dance. ''I'm so sorry. I didn't know. I blamed you. I thought you'd deliberately set out to hurt me. I had no idea what happened to you that night.''

His jaw tight and his body rigid, Jake bounded up from the sofa. He began pacing in front of her. ''By the time my father came for me, it was too late. Maybe it would have been different if he'd come years earlier, when I was just a boy, but those teen years had been hard. I don't consciously think about those days much, but I'll never forget the constant feeling of not belonging, of being an outcast, with no real parents to rely on. Of worrying every single time I messed up, the way young boys do, if I would be shipped off again to another town, another strange home. That's always with me, Cassie.''

Cassie wanted to wrap her arms around him and hug the pain away, but Jake was a man now, not a small boy. And he stood with tight control, his body relaying that he didn't need her sympathy, only her understanding. Jake was as prideful as John T., and that could be their undoing. Both were stubborn to a fault, but she contended that without a doubt, both men had hearts of gold that had been inadvertently buried under layers of misunderstanding, mistrust and mistakes.

Cassie stood up and went to him. She looked him in the eyes, searching and hoping to get through to him. ''I can only imagine how you felt, Jake. But things are different now. A good deal of time has passed. It heals.''

''Maybe one day.'' He didn't sound convinced. ''But at least you know I didn't deliberately stand you up. I didn't mean to hurt you that night.''

Cassie waved it off. ''That doesn't seem important now. What's important is that you made a good life for yourself. That you survived it all and became a wonderful man.''

''Wonderful, huh? How wonderful?'' He grinned and a dangerous gleam in his eyes returned, hot and steamy. Cassie knew that Jake had tired of the topic and their serious conversation was over. There'd be no more talk of the past, no more talk of forgiveness, at least for now.

Cassie tilted her head and paused coyly. ''Pretty darn wonderful.''

Jake spread his hands around her waist, bringing her close. He took in oxygen, a soulful breath of reined-in desire. ''Let's have breakfast in bed.''

Cassie couldn't deny him, she never really could, but especially now that he'd given her a glimpse into his past, she felt closer to him than ever. Her heart and her body both craved him. She found she was hungry for Jake in the most elemental way. "Let's."

Thirteen

––––––

"**C**ongratulations! You were great out there." Cassie greeted Jake at the gate with a big kiss moments after he'd made his victory lap around the perimeter of the stadium, with Shadow prancing and lapping up the attention. Jake's fellow competitors had eyed Cassie with interest, then let out whoops and hollers when she landed that kiss on his mouth. Jake only smiled. Eat your heart out, boys, he thought. She's mine.

Or she will be, once I figure her out.

Cassie waited for him patiently while he signed autographs at tables set up inside the arena for the fans. Jake wanted to get Cassie alone again, but it was nearing time to leave, their private time together almost over. He didn't know what tomorrow would bring. They'd had a great weekend yet Jake wasn't sure he was any closer to getting Cassie to agree to marry him than before they'd come here.

"There you go, Samuel," he said to a youngster he assumed was close to twelve, handing him the signed rodeo program. "Nice meeting you."

"Nice meeting you, sir. I'm planning on being a calf roper myself. My pa's fixing to teach me better. I've been practicing for two years now and he says soon I'm gonna be good enough to enter the junior rodeo. Did your pa teach you?"

"Nope. I taught myself. But it's better if you've got someone behind you, to teach you. If you're willing to work real hard, and keep practicing, you'll do just fine. You just listen up when your pa gives you advice."

The boy nodded briskly. "I will, sir. I hope you win the national finals."

"Thanks, I hope so, too. But I'll be back again next year, no matter what." Jake shook the boy's hand. "Well, good luck, Samuel."

Cassie stepped up then, her face thoughtful, her green eyes pensive. Jake stood and took her hand. "Come on. I'm all through here."

He led her to the corrals where his horses were penned up, noting that Cassie had become unusually quiet. Jake let her be. One thing he was beginning to learn about pregnant women, they had their moods. And pregnant or not, Cassie hadn't been an easy woman for him to understand anyway. "C'mon, ladies," he said to his horses. "Time to get packed up. We're heading home."

Home. Jake never felt at home at Anderson Ranch so the words didn't soothe, but made him edgy. He wished he could keep on the road, with Cassie by his side. That wasn't possible, of course. He'd have to leave again, alone. It was his life. But a gnawing twitch in his gut told him something was wrong. Real wrong. Cassie hadn't spoken a word.

A short time later, with the horses all set in the trailer and Cassie buckled in, Jake hit the road, his Dodge Ram kicking up rodeo dust. The balmy air brought heat, causing moisture to break out on his skin. Jake turned on the air conditioner and once they were on the interstate, he turned to look at Cassie. "I'm real glad you came with me, Cassie."

She cast him a small smile and nodded.

"Everything all right?" he asked, wondering now if she wasn't feeling well. Maybe the heat was getting to her or maybe they'd overdone it this weekend. They'd spent more time *in* bed, than out. Jake had tried damn hard not to let his desire get out of control, but it hadn't been easy. Not with Cassie. There was something special about her that had him tied up in knots.

"I'm fine, Jake. I was just thinking about what you said to that boy today."

"Samuel? The last autograph I signed?"

"Yes. You were so supportive. You told him to practice and take his father's advice. Did you ever have that with John T? Did he ever try to give you advice when you were learning?"

Jake took a deep breath. He didn't want to get into this. He didn't like dredging up the past. But Cassie seemed bent on asking her questions. He spoke honestly. "He tried. He had experience with the rodeo, but I—"

"You wanted to do it all on your own," Cassie finished for him, her tone far from understanding. She had no business judging him. She had no clue what it'd been like for him back then, trying to fit in at the ranch, but never knowing how, because he'd never fit in anyplace else before.

"Yeah, that's right," he said. "I'd learned by then that I couldn't rely on anyone. John T. tried for about a week, but I made it clear I didn't want his help or anyone else's. The success I have now, is all my own."

"You have no one to share it with, Jake. What good is that?"

"I don't need anyone to share it with."

Cassie lowered her gaze and spoke quietly. "I know."

"Dammit, Cassie. Don't turn this all around. Don't make this about you and me." Anger simmered in his gut. He didn't want to end their weekend on a sour note. Yet he didn't need this from Cassie, not now. Not ever. She would just have to accept him the way that he was.

"Have you ever invited your father to one of your rodeos?"

Jake snorted. "Are you kidding? He's not interested."

"No, I'm not kidding," she said so adamantly that Jake turned to look at her. She, too, turned so that her body faced him, but there was something remote in her eyes, a look that spoke of indecision. She bit down on her lower lip, pulling it in. At any other time Jake would have thought the move seductive, but right now he knew something was stirring up in her pretty head.

"What?" he asked, wondering if he really wanted to know the answer.

She hesitated a long moment, then, as if she'd finally made up her mind, she spoke her piece. "What if I told you that John T. has come to watch you compete? Many times."

Jake's mouth dropped open and he mentally had to shake his head. What was Cassie saying? Did she actually know this for a fact? Jake had trouble believing she knew what she was talking about. "Darlin', I'd say you are sorely mistaken."

"Maybe I shouldn't be telling you this, Jake. But it's true. John T. confided in me weeks ago."

A pulse beat out a hasty rhythm in his neck. Jake swore under his breath. Cassie had come into his life and turned it upside down. But now she was telling him something he was sure couldn't be true. "I don't believe it."

"I wouldn't lie."

"No, not you. I don't believe him. He's just trying to win your sympathy, Cassie."

"He was there in Colorado, when your horse threw a shoe. He was there when you won your first ever go-round. He was there to see you take Rookie of the Year honors, Jake."

A shudder went through Jake's body. He had to know the truth of it, because he'd never once thought John T. had any use for his career. He'd been hell-bent on getting Jake to work the ranch with him. "Why?"

Cassie smiled sadly. "Why? Do you really have to ask? Jake, you're his son. He's proud of you."

"He never told me."

"Would you have wanted him there? Would you have welcomed him?"

"Hell no!" The words rushed out of his mouth fast, giving Cassie reason to shake her head.

"John T. has as much pride as you do. Rejection doesn't set well with anyone, but especially with a prideful man."

"Damn." Jake couldn't think of anything else to say. He spent the remainder of the trip deep in thought, too shocked, too full of pent-up anger and confused emotion to make casual conversation. Once they arrived at the ranch, Jake parked the truck in front of the guest house.

Cassie turned to him, her gaze solemn and questioning. "What will you do if you win the championship in December?"

The baby was due around the holiday time. For Jake it meant that he might achieve his longtime goal and become a father in the very same month. "What would I do? A man can't win too many championships, Cassie. I'd go back, just like I told the boy today. No matter what. It's what I do.''

Cassie nodded, regret evident in her eyes. It was the same sort of look he'd witnessed in his wife's eyes while they lived in the shortest recorded marriage in recent Carson Valley history. "I see."

Another shudder waved its way down Jake's body. Cassie didn't see. She didn't know his life. He thought that they would become closer on this trip, but judging by the look on her face and the tone of her voice, Jake feared the opposite to be true. Cassie hadn't been wooed at all. She hadn't fallen victim to his charms. She hadn't jumped with joy at his proposals. Clearly she didn't understand him or the life he chose to lead.

And she confused the hell out of him with her revelations, her questions, and the look of disappointment he found too often on her pretty face. Everything Jake thought to be true was now muddied up in his mind. It was as if he'd been blinded in a dust storm, only to open his eyes, not knowing if what he was seeing was truth or some false mirage. He found himself wrapped up, spun in a web, tangled with thoughts that wove around him in an intricate pattern that he couldn't undo. Was it truth or mirage? How would he ever untangle himself and come out whole and in one piece? The survivor in him, for the first time in a very long time, didn't actually know.

Jake left Cassie at her door, his mind a million miles away. He couldn't bear to see that look in her eyes another minute. He couldn't bear to hear the disappointed tone in her voice. He couldn't deal with her right now.

He had his own troubles to face.

Cassie sat next to John T. in his study, going over some accounts that were past due. John T. knew his clients well, which ones were in dire straits and which were just lazy about settling up. Cassie had come to rely on his judgment and his expertise. When he leaned back in his tufted leather wing chair, Cassie relaxed, too. She didn't want to tire him out.

In typical John T. fashion he stared at her belly, with no attempt to be subtle. "How's the baby doing?"

"Great. I'm happy to report." She patted her stomach, giving it a loving rub. "I think I'm beginning to feel movement."

John T.'s gaze widened. "That so?"

"Well, I know it's a bit early, but yes, I think so. I feel little flutters."

"And Jake? Does he know?"

Cassie grimaced. She hadn't seen much of Jake lately. Ever since their weekend together, weeks ago, he'd come over a few times to say hello but he'd been distant at best. He had issues to deal with and Cassie had only hoped he was doing just that, dealing with them. She hoped he was doing some serious thinking. "No. I haven't seen much of him this week."

This time John T. grimaced. "Pretty soon, none of us will see much of him. It's almost July, otherwise known as Christmastime for the rodeo. From before Independence Day on, there's more rodeo events to be had, more money to be made and more points to earn. Most cowboys don't see a day at home during that time."

"Oh." Cassie couldn't keep the dejection out of her voice. As much as she wanted Jake to take stock of his life, as much as she hoped she'd made a dent in his hard-edged armor, she had also missed him. Now it seemed as though she wouldn't be seeing him for another month or so. And even fatherhood wouldn't keep him home from the rodeo.

He'd stated plainly that next year would be more of the same.

Thoughts filtered in that Cassie had consistently tried to banish from her mind. Would she and her baby always come second place with Jake? Would he abandon her time and again for the sake of a championship? Would he continue to deny his proper place as heir to the ranch? But most important, would he continue to shield his heart from her?

Cassie didn't know if she could play second fiddle again. It was too much to ask. She and the baby deserved more.

"Want me to speak to him when he gets back?" John T. offered.

"No. That's not necessary. He's doing what he has to do." Cassie didn't want to be the driving wedge between Jake and his father. She'd learned from Lottie that Jake had confronted John T. about his coming to the rodeo to see him compete. Jake had wanted to know the truth and the two had butted heads. What might have been an earnest reckoning had turned into a stubborn battle of wills. Cassie had blamed herself and apologized to John T. for letting the proverbial cat out of the bag. It seemed that all of her attempts to get the two closer failed. Cassie couldn't help feeling somewhat responsible. "Where is he this time?"

John T. scratched his head. "I think that boy muttered something about Denver before he took off yesterday."

So Jake was gone again. Cassie sighed then leaned back and stretched, lifting her arms high overhead. She'd been sitting in the chair for almost an hour and suddenly, she felt stiff all over.

John T. smiled. "You need some exercise. And I promised to the doctor I'd walk two miles everyday." John T. stood, reaching for her hand. "Why don't you join me? Sure would like the company."

Cassie bounded out of the chair, taking up his hand and his offer. "Sounds good to me."

Three hours later Cassie rested her head on the pillow in her hospital bed—the events of the past afternoon rushing by like a spiraling cyclone. One minute she was having a pleasant walk with John T. up on the south pasture, the next she was stumbling over a rock and falling down a three-foot slope. She'd righted herself quickly, but then the cramps had started instantly...and the bleeding. Cassie had doubled over in pain. She'd never known fear like that before. She'd never been gripped with such intense emotion. She'd prayed and prayed for her baby. The fall hadn't been that bad, she'd thought at first, but then she'd felt something terribly wrong and panic had seized her.

She'd been rushed to the hospital, John T. and Lottie by her side. Thank God her friends had been there.

"John T. is trying to get in touch with Jake. So far he hasn't been able to reach him. But don't you worry, honey, we'll catch up with him." Lottie squeezed her hand gently.

Cassie closed her eyes. *Hold on, Cassie. Don't lose it. Everything's going to be fine. The doctor says the baby isn't in any danger. The cramping and bleeding have stopped. All is well. You heard the baby's heartbeats just a minute ago.*

But Cassie wanted Jake. She wanted to see him, to have him hold her in his arms. She needed him right now, more than she ever had before. The doctor had given her news she desperately wanted to share with Jake. Where was he? It had been hours since the fall. Was he competing? How long before he would get the message and call?

"The doctor says the baby is just fine."

"Thank God, Lottie. I've never been so frightened in my life." Cassie lay a protective, soothing hand on her stomach.

''It was such a freak accident. I don't know what I would have done if the baby...'' Tears clouded her eyes and Cassie couldn't speak for a moment. ''I wish Jake was here.''

Lottie smiled reassuringly. ''He's a good man, Cassie. He'll be in touch. Don't you worry. Now, get some rest. If all goes well, the doctor says he'll release you in the morning.''

Jake was a good man, Cassie thought lovingly. She needed him. He'll call as soon as he gets the message.

Cassie closed her eyes peacefully, thankful for all the good things in her life, and finally allowed sleep to claim her.

Fourteen

Jake entered his hotel room, glancing at the clock with a frown. Damn, he'd stayed out past midnight, nursing one drink at the bar, listening to the band and shooting the breeze with the guys. He'd never been one to indulge, but lately he found he needed to keep his mind off one gorgeous redhead. She'd been entering his thoughts too often these days, making him question his life, making him uncomfortable with doubt.

But at least he had the good sense not to overdo before the finals tomorrow. Hangovers don't bode well when you're racing to rope a calf. And that's another thing, ever since he met up with Cassie, he'd questioned his lot in life. Just today, as he was looping the rope overhead, ready to make the toss, an uncanny notion filtered in.

This is a fool way to earn a living.

Jake resented that thought as much as he questioned the why of it. He had Cassie Munroe on the brain.

Jake sat down on his bed and tossed off his boots. As he began unbuttoning his shirt, he glanced over to see the telephone light blinking. He lifted the receiver and followed the directions, getting three messages, all from John T., his craggy voice elevated and more than slightly panicked.

Jake listened, his heart thumping hard in his chest.

''Cassie took a fall… She was rushed to the hospital… They're taking tests….''

Jake only half listened to the rest of the messages, his mind working overtime. Good Lord, Cassie had been hurt. She'd been bleeding. She'd been taken to the hospital. Jake had to speak with her. He had to know she was all right. And the baby. Their baby. How did the baby fare in all of this? Stark fear entered his heart. His body physically shook. He was so far away, too far to get to her right away. Damn. He needed to see her.

Since meeting Cassie he had struggled with emotions too raw and deep to name. He'd fought his feelings for her, just as he'd fought his father. With deep, soulful intensity. He'd been bitter and angry and afraid. Yes, afraid to feel anything for the two people in his life that meant the most to him. He'd had a lousy childhood, but his life since coming to the ranch hadn't been bad. It could have been better, had he allowed it. But ingrained hostility and apprehension had entered into the mix and Jake had put up walls to protect himself.

But all that was over now. He needed Cassie in his life. And it took an accident to knock him upside the head, proving once and for all how much she really did mean to him. He couldn't keep up the battle, the price of losing Cassie, far too high. He'd lost, or had he won?

Yes. He'd won, because he loved Cassie.

He could say it now, and damn the consequences. He had to speak with her. He had to hear her voice and own up to the truth. His truth. He had to tell her she would never play second fiddle again.

But the hospital wouldn't let his calls go through. Of course, it was too late. They wouldn't wake her. She needed to rest.

Jake took up his keys and packed his belongings quickly. He had a few things to attend to before leaving, then he'd drive all night to see Cassie in person.

And tell her what was in his heart.

It was late in the afternoon when Jake finally pulled inside the gates of the ranch. He'd stopped to telephone ahead to find that Cassie had been released from the hospital. That must be a good sign, he thought. She was home.

But when Jake knocked on her door, oddly, no one answered. Jake walked over to the main house, hoping that Lottie and John T. were busy pampering Cassie. Maybe they were having an early dinner. That sounded good. After the long drive, Jake was famished, for Cassie and for a hot plate of food. He needed both right now.

He met John T. on the front porch. "You're a little too late, son."

Jake's heart skipped a beat. "Where is she?"

"Gone. I couldn't stop her. She got a clean bill of health from the doctor. Thank God, for that. But when she didn't hear from you, she took off. Going back to Los Angeles to work with her brother. Nearly broke my heart to see her go, Jake. Why the hell didn't you call her at least?"

Anger surfaced, but Jake tamped it down. That was the old Jake, the one who had too many defenses for his own good. And he'd recognized what he'd done to Cassie all this time. It was the same thing he'd tried to do to John T. He'd driven her away. He could see that now. He knew that she hadn't abandoned him, but rather the opposite. He had abandoned her. And he was willing to do whatever it took to make things right. "I didn't get your messages until after midnight. I tried calling the hospital, but they wouldn't put me through, so I packed up and drove all night."

John T. scratched his head. "Cassie kept saying she wasn't going play second fiddle anymore. She's through with you, Jake. She doesn't think you care anything for her."

"I love her, Dad."

John T. blinked, a look of shock on his face, and Jake didn't know if it was his admission of love or the fact that he'd called him *Dad* that had caused it.

But John T. smiled, a genuine, heartfelt smile that Jake finally could return. They grinned together. "I've got things to say to you and a plan for us to work at the ranch, but I've got to get Cassie back first. How long ago did she leave?"

"She couldn't leave without saying goodbye to Lottie. If you hurry, and take the shortcut over the canyon, you might catch her on the road up by Lottie's house."

"I'll follow her all the way to Los Angeles if I have to. That woman's the best thing in my life."

"Well, now, we finally agree. You go after her, son. Good luck."

Jake nodded then took a step, then another, toward his father. He wrapped his arms around John T. and gave him a brief hug. "Thanks, Dad."

John T.'s eyes misted up and his voice went soft. "You go on now. Bring her home."

Cassie dried her eyes with a tissue Lottie had given her. "This is so hard, Lottie," she said, ignoring the tea Lottie had put out and the blueberry muffins. She was too broken-hearted to eat or drink. All she'd done today was cry. She sat at Lottie's kitchen table, willing herself to get up and leave. She had a long drive ahead of her. She couldn't bear to stay at the ranch another day, knowing how little she meant to Jake. Knowing he hadn't even bothered to call her. "I hate saying goodbye to you. It was hard enough seeing the look of pain on John T.'s face. I'm taking his grandchild away. But I swear to you both, you'll see us, whenever you want."

"Oh, honey. Are you sure you want to leave? Maybe, if you stayed on a little while longer, things would work out."

Sadly, Cassie shook her head. "No. I have to be strong. I can't live here, knowing that I'm just an afterthought to Jake. I was in the hospital most of the morning and he never called. He didn't call the house, either. He was too busy with the rodeo. It's all very clear to me now. I thought that if I loved him enough, if I proved to him, that John T. truly did care for him, that Jake would finally come around. But his wounds are too deep, I'm afraid. I couldn't get through to him. So, now," Cassie said, rising slowly, "I have to go."

Cassie hugged her friend tight and Lottie walked her outside. "Call me when you arrive, okay?"

"I will. I promise." Cassie got into her car and started the engine, waving a last goodbye to Lottie.

"You're coming to our wedding."

"I wouldn't miss it," Cassie said, smiling through a cloud of tears as she drove off down the road and out the gate, leaving her friends and heart behind.

Jake's luck was holding. Mounted on Shadow up on a hill, he peered down at the road. Cassie's neon-yellow bug of a car was stopped alongside a tree, apparently out of gas. The woman in dark sunglasses, tight jeans and black boots walked with purpose down the road, the slight bulge of her stomach against the flow of her soft-pink shirt bringing a wave of warmth to his heart.

"C'mon, Shadow. Looks like the lady needs rescuing." Jake made his way down a steep path, halting his mount just a few yards from Cassie's approach.

He reined in Shadow. "Need some help?"

"No thanks, cowboy." She walked right past him. But he didn't miss her look of stunned surprise before she plastered on a stone face.

Jake rode up ahead, dismounted and waited for her. He jutted out his arms in surrender, much like a man being held at gunpoint, although Jake had to admit Cassie's weapons were far more dangerous. "I know, I know. You don't need a white knight."

"That's right. That's not what I need." Cassie removed her sunglasses, pointing them at him, and those incredible green eyes, once again, nearly knocked him to his knees. He took a long, slow look at her, grateful that she appeared so healthy. And his heart pounded wildly—his love for her slamming hard against his chest. "I'm through with white knights. So you can climb back up on your horse."

"Not a chance, honey. I've set things right with my father and I intend to do the same with you. Drove all night to see you, so I'm not about to let you go."

Jake untied a bag from the back of his saddle and handed it to her. Looking deep into her eyes, he said softly, "Unwrap it."

Puzzled, Cassie maneuvered an object out of the leather satchel. "It's a…fiddle."

With pride, Jake announced, "It's a Cremona, Italian-made, and I'm told the best in the line. There's a country player up in Denver with a pocketful of cash right now that has got to be wondering why on earth a crazy cowboy begged him for his fiddle in the middle of the night. But, it's all yours, sweetheart. You'll never have to play second fiddle again.''

''Jake, I don't under—''

''I've quit the rodeo, Cassie. Gonna work the ranch with my father. Besides, can't see tying up a calf when I've got me a girl like you to rope in. Gonna make you mine even if I have to hog-tie you.''

Cassie looked at him, then the fiddle. A wave of warmth spread through her body. Jake had come for her. He'd made amends with his father. But what was he saying, exactly? She wished the cowboy would simply say what was on his mind. ''Jake?''

Jake took the fiddle from her hands and untied a brilliant diamond ring from one of the strings. She'd been too stunned, too jolted, by Jake and his showing up here to notice the ring of gold on the fiddle.

''You're first in my heart, Cassie. Always will be. Baby or no baby, I want you in my life.'' With slow calculation Jake slid the ring on her finger, the fit, perfect. ''I love you, Cassie Munroe. I love you with all of my heart. You've got to believe me because I've never said those words to anyone. And I mean them with everything I've got inside.''

Cassie stared deeply into his eyes and found truth there. And love. She did believe him. Jake loved her. Joy she'd never known entered into her heart and a sense of peace enveloped her with amazing clarity. ''Jake. I love you, too. So much.'' Her eyes burned with unshed, happy tears. Their child, too, responded in kind. ''Oh, I think the baby just kicked.''

With reverence, Jake laid his hand on her stomach and she witnessed his open expression, free of hurt and pain, perhaps for the first time in his life. ''It's a miracle, honey.''

Cassie smiled wide and stated with certainty, ''Two miracles, Jake.''

Jake tipped his head sideways, his dark, loving gaze meeting hers. "You mean, because we're getting married and having a baby?"

Cassie shook her head. "No, sweetheart. Because we're having two babies. Twins! I just found out yesterday."

Jake hesitated a moment, absorbing what she'd just confided. Then he let out a loud whoop of joy. "Twins?" He grabbed Cassie gently, lifting her and spinning her around, his laughter mingling with hers. "Twins," he said again, pressing his lips to hers in a deep, soulful, passionate kiss. "Two babies at once. You're always full of surprises. God, I love you."

"I love you, too, Jake. But don't forget we've got another five months to go."

"That's just fine with me, sweetheart. John T.'s been making wedding plans since the day you showed up at his door. He'll be tickled to know we're getting hitched and there's two babies on the way."

Cassie stroked Jake's cheek softly, her heart filled with happiness for him, for all of them. "You're finally going to have a family, Jake. John T., Lottie, the babies and me, we all love you. We'll be your family."

Jake kissed the soft side of her hand. "I'm a lucky man."

Then Cassie took a mischievous tone, lifting her brows in anticipation. "And what was that you said about roping me in?"

A grin pulled at his lips. He pulled her even closer in his embrace, fitting her soft body into the groove of his hard one, leaving no doubt where his mind and body had drifted. "I've got enough good moves to keep you tied up for a lifetime, honey."

* * * * * *

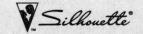

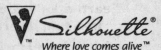

If you enjoyed what you just read,
then we've got an offer you can't resist!

Take 2 bestselling
love stories FREE!
Plus get a FREE surprise gift!

Clip this page and mail it to Silhouette Reader Service™

IN U.S.A.	IN CANADA
3010 Walden Ave.	P.O. Box 609
P.O. Box 1867	Fort Erie, Ontario
Buffalo, N.Y. 14240-1867	L2A 5X3

YES! Please send me 2 free Silhouette Desire® novels and my free surprise gift. After receiving them, if I don't wish to receive anymore, I can return the shipping statement marked cancel. If I don't cancel, I will receive 6 brand-new novels every month, before they're available in stores! In the U.S.A., bill me at the bargain price of $3.57 plus 25¢ shipping and handling per book and applicable sales tax, if any*. In Canada, bill me at the bargain price of $4.24 plus 25¢ shipping and handling per book and applicable taxes**. That's the complete price and a savings of at least 10% off the cover prices—what a great deal! I understand that accepting the 2 free books and gift places me under no obligation ever to buy any books. I can always return a shipment and cancel at any time. Even if I never buy another book from Silhouette, the 2 free books and gift are mine to keep forever.

225 SDN DNUP
326 SDN DNUQ

Name	(PLEASE PRINT)	
Address	Apt.#	
City	State/Prov.	Zip/Postal Code

* Terms and prices subject to change without notice. Sales tax applicable in N.Y.
** Canadian residents will be charged applicable provincial taxes and GST.
  All orders subject to approval. Offer limited to one per household and not valid to current Silhouette Desire® subscribers.
  ® are registered trademarks of Harlequin Books S.A., used under license.

DES02   ©1998 Harlequin Enterprises Limited

Silhouette®

Desire®

**is proud to present
an exciting new miniseries from**

KATHIE DeNOSKY

Lonetree Ranchers

On the Lonetree Ranch, passions explode
under Western skies for these
handsome-but-hard-to-tame bachelors.

In August 2003—
LONETREE RANCHERS: BRANT

In October 2003—
LONETREE RANCHERS: MORGAN

In December 2003—
LONETREE RANCHERS: COLT

Available at your favorite retail outlet.

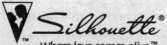

Silhouette®

Where love comes alive™

COMING NEXT MONTH

#1525 THE LIBRARIAN'S PASSIONATE KNIGHT—
Cindy Gerard
Dynasties: The Barones
Love was the last thing on Daniel Barone's mind…until he rescued
Phoebe Richards from her pushy ex one fateful night. The shy librarian
was undeniably appealing, with her delectable curves and soft brown eyes, but
had this sexy bachelor finally met the woman who'd tame his playboy heart?

#1526 BILLIONAIRE BACHELORS: GRAY—
Anne Marie Winston
After Gray MacInnes underwent a heart transplant, he began having
flashes of strange memories…which led him to his donor's elegant widow,
Catherine Thorne, and her adorable son. His memories of endless nights
with her in his arms soon became a breathtaking reality, but Gray only
hoped Catherine would forgive him once she learned his true identity.

#1527 THE HEART OF A STRANGER—Sheri WhiteFeather
Lone Star Country Club
When she found a handsome stranger unconscious on her ranch,
Lourdes Quinterez had no idea her life was about to change forever.
She nursed the man back to health only to learn he had amnesia. Though
Juan Guapo, as she called him, turned out to be Ricky Mercado, former
mob boss, Lourdes would stand by the man who'd melted her heart with his
smoldering kisses.

#1528 LONETREE RANCHERS: BRANT—Kathie DeNosky
Never able to resist a woman in need, bullfighter Brant Wakefield was happy
to help lovely heiress Annie Devereaux when she needed protection from a
dangerous suitor. But soon they were falling head over heels for each other, and
though Brant feared they were too different to make it work, his passion for her
would not be denied.…

#1529 DESERT WARRIOR—Nalini Singh
Family pressure had forced Mina Coleridge to reject her soul mate four
years ago. Now circumstances had brought Tariq Zamanat back to her—as
her husband! Though he shared his body with her, his heart was considered
off-limits. But Mina had lost Tariq once before, and *this* time she was
determined to hold on to her beloved sheik.

#1530 HAVING THE TYCOON'S BABY—Anna DePalo
The Baby Bank
All Liz Donovan needed to realize her dream of having a baby was a trip
to the fertility clinic. But then the unthinkable happened—her teenage crush,
millionaire Quentin Whittaker, proposed a marriage of convenience! It wasn't
long before Liz was wondering if making a baby the old-fashioned way could
lead to the family of her dreams.

SDCNM0703

Love Inspired
SUSPENSE

TITLES AVAILABLE NEXT MONTH

Don't miss these four stories in May

REQUEST YOUR FREE BOOKS!
2 FREE RIVETING INSPIRATIONAL NOVELS
PLUS 2 FREE MYSTERY GIFTS

Love Inspired®
SUSPENSE

YES! Please send me 2 FREE Love Inspired® Suspense novels and my 2 FREE mystery gifts. After receiving them, if I don't wish to receive any more books, I can return the shipping statement marked "cancel." If I don't cancel, I will receive 4 brand-new novels every month and be billed just $3.99 per book in the U.S. or $4.74 per book in Canada, plus 25¢ shipping and handling per book and applicable taxes, if any*. That's a savings of 20% off the cover price! I understand that accepting the 2 free books and gifts places me under no obligation to buy anything. I can always return a shipment and cancel at any time. Even if I never buy another book from Steeple Hill, the two free books and gifts are mine to keep forever.

123 IDN EL5H   323 IDN ELQH

Name	(PLEASE PRINT)	
Address		Apt. #
City	State/Prov.	Zip/Postal Code

Signature (if under 18, a parent or guardian must sign)

Order online at www.LoveInspiredSuspense.com

Or mail to Steeple Hill Reader Service™:
IN U.S.A.: P.O. Box 1867, Buffalo, NY 14240-1867
IN CANADA: P.O. Box 609, Fort Erie, Ontario L2A 5X3

Not valid to current Love Inspired Suspense subscribers.

Want to try two free books from another series?
Call 1-800-873-8635 or visit www.morefreebooks.com

* Terms and prices subject to change without notice. NY residents add applicable sales tax. Canadian residents will be charged applicable provincial taxes and GST. This offer is limited to one order per household. All orders subject to approval. Credit or debit balances in a customer's account(s) may be offset by any other outstanding balance owed by or to the customer. Please allow 4 to 6 weeks for delivery.

Your Privacy: Steeple Hill is committed to protecting your privacy. Our Privacy Policy is available online at www.eHarlequin.com or upon request from the Reader Service. From time to time we make our lists of customers available to reputable firms who may have a product or service of interest to you. If you would prefer we not share your name and address, please check here. ☐

LISUS07